Praise for The Lamoille Stories

"Bill Schubart's Vermont stories of a mostly forgotten time and place are fresh, authentic, funny in places and sad in others. He knows his corner of the Green Mountains inside and out and writes with honesty and grace about its people."
—Howard Frank Mosher, author of *Disappearances, Marie Blythe* and *On Kingdom Mountain*

"Bill Schubart's stories are Vermont's answer to Chaucer's *Canterbury Tales*: larger than life, triumphantly over-the-top, by turns erudite and savagely, raucously funny. No good soul, no matter how low on the social ladder, is beneath Schubart's fond notice; no lout, no matter how highly placed, escapes his lacerating wit. People drink in these stories, folks. They drink and occasionally they damage their homes and cars and boots and lifelong local reputations as a result. But in Schubart's universe, such things happen, and such people remain loved. Laughed at certainly, but loved just the same."
—Philip Baruth, Vermont State Legislator and author of *Brothers Boswell* and The *Millennium Shows*

"These are fast becoming my favorite stories. Bill Schubart captures something of Vermont that many of us barely remember, and others may never experience. Each of the *Lamoille Stories* is a unique experience—lovingly told, with insight, pathos, and especially humor. You'll read them again and again."
—Joseph A. Citro, author of *Passing Strange* and *Lake Monsters*

"Neither the postcard image of Vermont nor the Norman Rockwell version fits the fiction of Bill Schubart. His spot-on authentic folk tales of small town pranksters and tough cases, drunkards and darlings, swerve from comedy to heartbreak like a winding back road. Ultimately, like the old man hand-digging the grave of his wife of 70 years, these stories possess a kindness, wisdom and dignity that make them well worth the read."
—Stephen Kiernan, author of *The Curiosity* and *Last Rights*

The Lamoille Stories II

Also by Bill Schubart:
The Lamoille Stories 978-0-9897121-0-1
Fat People 978-0-615-39751-1
Panhead 978-0-9834852-6-1
I Am Baybie 978-0-9834852-9-2
Photographic Memory 978-0-9834852-8-5

Published September 2014 by Magic Hill Press, LLC
144 Magic Hill Rd, Hinesburg, VT 05461
www.MagicHillPress.com
MSRP: $15.00 PB // $9.99 EB

As recounted by Claire Hancock
Front Cover Photograph by Richard Brown
Typesetting by Alex Ching
Edited by Ruth Sylvester

ISBN 978-0-9897121-3-2
Library of Congress Control Number: 2013958455

Publisher's Cataloging-in-Publication
Schubart, Bill, 1945-
The Lamoille stories. II, Willy's beer garden
20 new tales from Vermont / Bill Schubart.
pages 132 m
Includes index.
     LCCN 2013958455
     ISBN 978-0-9897121-3-2
     ISBN 978-0-9897121-4-9
     ISBN 978-0-9897121-5-6

     1. Lamoille County (Vt.)--Fiction. 2. Vermont--
     Fiction. I. Title. II. Title: Willy's beer garden
     and 20 new tales from Vermont.

          PS3619.C467L36 2014   813'.6
          QBI14-600028

Author's Note: *Lila's Bucket* appears in the original edition of *Lamoille Stories*. *Lost Key* and *Bakin' for the Bacon* also appear as chapters in *Photographic Memory*.

The Lamoille Stories II

Willy's Beer Garden and
20 New Tales from Vermont

Bill Schubart

Foreplay

We are our stories. Our stories entertain, instruct, and survive us. They morph in each telling and infuse listeners with their own stories. The best are told by master story tellers. My sister, Claire Hancock, is one of the best story tellers I know and many of these are stories she has told our family over the years. Others, I have retained from friends and still others, knitted out of yarns I heard as I tried to grow up.

I am a writer and so these twenty-one tales now arrive in print and join the twenty-two that appeared five years ago in the first volume of *Lamoille Stories*.

Apart from the family and friends from whom I have gathered these stories, I would like to thank those who have helped me frame them into a book: my editor, Ruth Sylvester, who does much more than copy-edit, correcting my arcane allusions to tractors and chainsaws when they are wrong and also, enhancing Vermont dialect, which she knows well. Thanks as well to Richard Brown, the world-class photographer who has captured the past and present essence of Vermont people and their working landscape. His photos grace both volumes of *The Lamoille Stories*.

Finally, thanks to the many childhood and current friends and families of Lamoille County who inspire, inhabit, and grace these fictional pages with the truth of their own stories.

The Stories

Lost Key and *Bakin' for the Bacon* also appear in *Photographic Memory*
**Lila's Bucket* appears in the original edition of *Lamoille Stories*

Lamoille County, Vermont

Willy's Beer Garden

THE FIRST TIME Willy Dyke showed up at his trailer dragging a case of Old Fitzgerald beer quarts instead of opening his sweaty wallet so his wife Ruby could fish out the cluster of hard-earned dollar bills was the last.

Willy watched as Ruby removed each bottle slowly from the corrugated hive and tapped it lightly with a ball peen hammer. Willy trembled as he watched the golden fluid running down the front steps of their trailer and the growing pile of brown glass shards.

Willy had been working since 7:30 that morning up at Art Weissner's, digging and setting the fence posts he'd creosoted the day before to enclose Art's daughter's new riding ring. Willy liked repetitive work. He knew what was expected and rarely had to ask directions. He was sought out in town because of his enthusiasm for jobs others turned down. Laying fence was his favorite. Digging grave holes was his least favorite. He didn't like cemeteries. Luckily, there was plenty of fence work in this community of waning dairy farmers and waxing equestrienne wives and daughters.

When asked about his hourly wage, Willy's response was always the same, "Whatever ya thinks I'se worth." A tough childhood had denied him any sense of self-worth and his earliest memories of asking for things were of being slapped and yelled at. His compensation varied from 85 cents an hour to as much as $1.50 and was usually inversely proportional to the wealth of the person hiring him. Trouble was, it was only rich folks that offered steady work. The wage variance did, however, give him latitude in what he surrendered to Ruby. Besides, in the spring, farmers vied for Willy's help mending pasture fence, and that was what he liked best.

The case of Old Fitz had cost him half his day's earnings. Ruby didn't make Willy open his wallet, so he could keep the $4.35 he had left. When the last bottle was broken, Ruby went inside and slammed the trailer door. Willy got a snow shovel and broom from the woodshed and cleaned up all the broken glass. The smell of almost four hundred ounces of beer seeping into the path leading up to his and Ruby's modest dwelling was heartbreaking.

The Dykes had lived along Cady's Creek for as long as anyone could remember. Their trailer sat on disputed marshland, about which neither claimant cared enough to hire a lawyer. The County Overseer of the Poor had suggested to Willy that he locate there because no owner was registered in the town records. The other option would have been National Forest land where several other poor families lived in deer camps and trailers, including Willy and Ruby's son, Junior.

Willy had had to clear a 350-yard swath of birch forest to get his trailer down there, towed behind Norbert Jackman's biggest International. Norbert used the tractor's bucket to level the trailer on a base of old railroad ties Willy had scavenged from the right-of-way of the defunct St. J. and L.C. rail line — now a bike and riding path.

The land was swampy all year but especially in the spring when the creek rose. The moldering ties eventually settled into the clay mire and the trailer assumed a significant tilt toward the creek. Ruby haunted Willy about fixing it but the birch trees had grown back and there was only a footpath to their home now, since they didn't own a car. A few years back, Willy had borrowed two five-ton bottle jacks from Fred Green in hopes of jacking it up and adding more rail ties on the downside. With Junior's help, Willy set the jacks on a base of ties and began jacking up the trailer. But the jacks only pushed the ties deeper into the soft clay and the trailer didn't budge. Hoping his and his son's efforts would satisfy Ruby, he'd let the matter rest.

The next time Willy bought a case of Old Fitz quarts, he was smarter. He drank two on the way home and stopped every 25 feet or so and buried a bottle with his posthole-digger along the path from the highway to his trailer. During an earlier job up at Shady Elms Cemetery, it was so hot he had had to down several quarts of Old Fitz to keep hydrated and, fearing Ruby might again notice the diminished wages, he'd scooped up a bunch of faded plastic flowers from the resting place of one Mildred Cohenny to bring home to mollify her. Ruby sensed the ruse and hurled the flowers at him, again slamming the trailer door in his face.

Not one to waste, Willy gathered them up and stashed them in the shed, knowing they, like everything else in there, would find a use some-day. They did. Over each buried quart, Willy inserted the stem of a plastic flower so as to remember its location when his thirst arose again.

Hiking back up from the creek with a creel full of browns and brookies, Judd Tremblay happened to notice this odd behavior. He couldn't for the life of him figure what Willy was doing burying bottles of beer and marking them with plastic flowers. It was known that Willy exhibited odd behav-ior when drinking and Judd saw the half- empty quart he carefully set down next to each new hole as he dug it. Judd wondered if Willy'd finally succumbed to wet brain and thought he was laying fence posts instead of burying full bottles of beer.

Knowing Willy, Judd thought little more of it and continued home to clean and fry up his fish in butter and scallions with some spring potatoes for supper. At dinner, he mentioned Willy's strange behavior to his wife, Melanie, and son, Luke.

"What you suppose Willy was thinkin'?" he asked.

"Maybe he's worried Probition'll come back," ventured Melanie as she pulled a fish bone from between her only two contiguous teeth. Luke said nothing.

Luke was a 15-year-old 8th grader. He resented being in class with kids two years his junior and was always working to curry favor with the high school boys, who welcomed him although they teased him for being in grade school. To make matters worse, Luke was almost six feet tall. Denny Kito-nis, a sophomore, was Luke's most indulgent friend and they often fished and hunted together when Denny wasn't working on his father's potato farm. The two had shared a number of misadventures since their first sep-aration, back in fourth grade, when Luke was kept back for the first time.

The most eventful was last summer when the boys had "borrowed" Doctor Phil's Ford Galaxy convertible for a joyride. This was not an alto-gether unusual event in a small town and usually overlooked by law enforcement if there was no damage and the vehicle owner worked out reparations with the malefactors, such as a year's worth of free car washes, lawn mowing, or snow shoveling. This joyride, however, got complicated when the boys picked up a couple of Hardwick girls hitchhiking along Route 15. When asked where they were headed, the girls answered, "where the beers are."

Luke turned off Route 15 and took the back road through Hardwood Flats over to Elmore so Denny could snag a couple of jugs of sap beer out of his father's root cellar. Then they made for Cady's Falls to go for a swim. One thing naturally led to another and, just before dawn, Luke parked the convertible on Congress Street a block away from Doctor Phil's large-frame Victorian home and office, to be discovered the next morning with an empty gas tank and evidence of a "joyride" in the form of a full ashtray and the rank smell of stale beer.

After questioning the usual truants, Officer Westley could find no useful leads and the matter subsided since no harm had been done to vehicle or property. Luke and Denny were in the clear and life went on as usual until Luke came home from school one day to find his mother in tears. When he came into the living room, she screamed at him, "You're no better than my ex-pecker," and threw down an official-looking paper. It was a citation charging him with rape.

He couldn't make any sense of the legalese and wasn't exactly sure what rape meant. Looking frantically at his mother, he said sullenly, "The sex part was her idea. We all drank some beer and she got real pushy, you know. I's the one was scared."

"Did you do it?"

"Yes, but she said she wanted to. She never said no. Fact she sort of showed me how. After awhile, I just got tired and she rolled over and said she didn't want to do it anymore and we stopped."

"Did you force yourself on her?"

"No, swear to God. She wanted to do it. I've only done it once before and still not sure what you're s'pose to do."

"You've done it before?"

"Well, once."

"With who?"

I'ain't tellin'."

"I know her?"

"Yup."

"Who, then?"

Ain't tellin'."

"You got yourself in big trouble now. The cops been here and you'll be going to court, if not reform school."

"But she started it."

"I don't care, you must'a finished it."

"Damn!"

The trial lasted an hour, just long enough for everyone in town to learn the details of the affair. Levi Smith, the Legal Aid attorney, cited the victim's deposition many times, while Judge Whitely struggled to maintain judicial composure.

"Course, we all thought we'd have some fun, you know. Ain't no harm in that, is there? Not like we never done it before. We was in the grass by the falls and we'd all had most of the strong beer. Not sure Denny and Lucy did it, but Luke and I did, but I soon realize there wan't no pleasure to be had from him. His thing-us was too little and I got bored. I think he did, too. But I finally said, 'No more' and stopped."

"Why did you think you were being raped?" the prosecuting attorney asked.

"Like I told you, there wan't no pleasure to it. It was too little."

Luke's family and friends were all in court to vouch for Luke's character and show support. Judge Cletus Whitely summoned the prosecution and defense to the bench and after some whispering they retired to chambers, emerging only a few minutes later. With one gavel blow, Judge Billings dismissed the charges. He lectured Luke sternly on car theft, consensual and non-consensual sex, and made clear that the police would be watching him. He then dismissed the court.

Details of the day's proceedings spread through town like a medieval plague. All agreed that Luke had atoned adequately in the courtroom for his poor judgment. It was, in fact, Luke's last run-in with the law.

Later in the fall, Luke was helping the town scapegrace, Pete Trepanier, change out the transmission in his Ford 8N tractor one afternoon and the two were chatting about various events in town. Pete forbore telling Luke about the new moniker his misadventure had earned him among the wags in town. Instead he talked about the spring salmon run in the Willoughby River and their favorite fishing spots. It was then that Luke volunteered the story of Willy's eccentric behavior burying quarts of beer on the path to his trailer. Pete suggested that perhaps Willy's years of drinking cheap beer and rotgut liquor might have affected his brain.

As it happened, Willy's ruse had been working just fine, although

Patch's Market no longer sold cases of 12 quart bottles. Like most outlets, they'd moved to cases of 24 -12- ounce bottles, so Willy's bottle burial chores doubled. Ruby still questioned her husband's paltry earnings on some days and chided him about demanding a better hourly wage, but she still hadn't discovered his buried cache or noticed the plastic flowers blooming in their woods.

Famous for his own pranks, like endlessly refilling Mr. Skiff's new VW with gas so he never ran out and bragged all over town how he got several hundred miles to the gallon, Pete kept thinking about Willy's eccentric behavior. First, he determined to see if the tale Lil' Luke told him was true.

Early one morning, Pete snuck down the path to Willy and Ruby's trailer looking for a plastic flower. He found one, dug it up and, sure enough, a few inches below the flower was a 12-ounce bottle of Old Fitz. Pete was surprised, as he'd remembered Willy drinking quarts. He replaced the bottle and left.

Over the weekend, Morris Treadway died and so did Mable Demus. That meant more grave digging for Willy.

On his way to the cemetery, He dug up a few bottles of beer to assuage the thirst he knew would overcome him in the heat. He pocketed the first bottle, but was surprised when the second was a quart. He thought nothing of it, as there were now probably thirty or forty bottles buried among the birches.

Willy always provided a full day's sober work and was happy just looking forward to downing several bottles sitting in the shade of a birch tree or along the creek before making the rest of his way home. Since they'd been given a used Admiral TV set, Ruby hardly ever left the trailer, so it was easy to escape Ruby's notice. Willy's only exception to this rule was digging graves. Willy often needed to brace himself against his malaise in the cemetery.

The following day, Willy worked at Denis Couture's putting in a white picket fence around their new camp up on Lake Elmore. After work, he hitchhiked and walked the final distance home, looking forward to three or four beers in the shade. To his great pleasure and surprise, the first beer he dug up was a quart, as was the second and the third. The following day, he buried another case in various locations in the woods, but he marked each burial site with a blue flower, vowing to dig up only those beers during the next few days so he wouldn't get confused about what he had buried, where, or when, as it had been at least a month since he'd buried any quarts.

To his surprise and elation, the three bottles he dug up the following day were all quarts. At first, he was worried that he had grown confused, although other details in his life and work seemed to have remained clear and he'd been offered more work than he could handle, especially among the horsey set. He decided to let the matter be and enjoy his good fortune.

Afraid of jinxing his good fortune, Willy kept mum about his beer garden and how he could plant a 12-ounce bottle of beer and within a few days harvest a quart.

But miracles eventually come to light. After augmenting his evening beers with a pint of blackberry brandy, Willy bragged to Junior of his gardening success, showing him how he could bury a 12-ouncer on Friday and dig up a 32-ouncer by Monday. Junior, equally amazed but far less reserved than his father, blabbed word of the miracle to his friend "Lil' Luke," with whom he was working at the Greaves Farm on third cutting.

Within days the whole town knew of the "miracle of Willy's beer garden" and Willy, to his horror, found people digging in his woods trying to confirm the story.

It all ended one night when the tale made it to Rene's bar in Eden where Pete was hanging out. Hearing the tale, Pete broke out in loud guffaws and bought the house a round and explained the miracle of Willy's beer garden to an eager audience.

Ruby was less amused than the towns-folk when she learned where Willy's wages had been going. She locked him out for several weeks. But Pete let him move into his cabin until Ruby, missing Willy's income, calmed herself and let him come home.

The Final Bid

AUCTIONS ELICIT MIXED reactions. The melancholy, whose homes or farms are being sold to strangers, don't share the excitement of those who have come from miles away to buy their chattels, house, or land at the lowest possible price.

Art Messier learned auctioneering from his father who'd made a killing during the Depression, selling off hill farms and homesteads for local bankers, who, to their chagrin, then discovered they were in the real estate business instead of the mortgage lending business. Like his father, Art had learned never to engage with the involuntary seller or his family. So when a kid would ask him if he or she could keep their bike or the calf they raised for 4H, Art could say, "Ask that man over there in the suit. It's okay with me if it's okay with him."

There were far fewer distress sales nowadays and most of Art's work was emptying out farms and houses for resale by people who had wearied of farm life, bought RVs, trailers, or cramped condos in Florida and fled hard work and winter to sit in an aluminum folding chair soaking up daily sunshine, paying lower taxes, counting liver spots, and gradually decaying.

Art's wife, Annie, handled the cash box and registered arriving bidders, who exchanged their driver's license for a pine paddle with a black number painted on it. His daughter, Jessica, recently arrested for shop-lifting a bathing suit, some hand drills, and a stud-finder from Sears, worked the selling area with her husky girlfriend, Maxine.

As a Herculon-upholstered Barcalounger "with a few stains" fell under the hammer for seven bucks, the girls wrestled a Mission oak dresser onto the riser for a full description and demonstration by Art of how easily the recently soaped drawers glided in and out and a brief digression on the emerging market for Mission furniture.

"Do I hear five dollars? Come on now, steal this piece. Don't make me give it away. Let's go! I hear five, do I hear seven? Come on, boys and girls. You know quality when you see it. Who'll gimme seven? I got five. Come on, who'll gimme six? Let's go. I ain't got all day. There, number 28. I got seven on you. This man knows quality when he sees it. Nobody else? Get 'cher paddle up. You boys can't get anything else up! Let's go. Don't let him steal it from you! Do I hear ten? Come on folks. It's getting warm up here. There, I got ten! Let me hear twelve! I got twelve, now fifteen. I got fifteen, Twenty? Give me twenty. Come on boys and girls. You'd pay fifty for this piece at an antique store. Let's go. I hear twenty. On you with the blue denim jacket at twenty... do I hear $25...Sold at twenty to number 34 in the back."

The sing-song undulations of Art's auction banter held the attention of the crowd as more furniture and appliances were muscled on stage by the two muscular girls. When the hammer came down, the girls would lower the sold item to the waiting hands of the high bidder who carried their new goods off to a cache near where they sat in a folding chair or next to their parked car. Annie kept track on a form of each item sold, the bidder's number, and the selling amount so at the end of the auction, each bidder would line up to pay with "hard cash" or "good check" to ransom their driver's license and get a stamped receipt for their purchases.

Mornings were usually dedicated to household goods. Tractors, farm implements, hand tools, and bargain boxes followed in that order over the course of the afternoon. The choice of goods coming under the hammer was carefully arranged to retain buyers for as much of the day as possible. Some came just to bid on a tractor or piece of furniture, but many came for the dollar bargain boxes that came up at the very end, mixing goods of marginal value into odd lots that sold for very little and made for the many bargain tales bidders would later tell jealous friends.

Lurlene and Frank's Fried Dough concession truck was parked back by Annie's folding table and served a steady line of folks buying coffee and fried dough in the morning; franks, burgers, and fries starting at 11, and back to coffee and fried dough in the afternoon. A wobbly condiment table sat under the awning near the ordering window where folks could douse fried snacks from pump-top gallon cans of ketchup, mustard and sweet relish, or add cinnamon from an aluminum shaker to their fried dough, white vinegar to their fries, or cream and sugar to their coffee. Frank and

Lurlene were not licensed to sell alcoholic beverages from their truck, although many beer-shaped brown bags appeared between knees of bidders who'd strolled past the back of the food trailer.

Pete Trepanier made a point of attending most farm auctions in the area with an eye to acquiring a dead or dying tractor to rebuild or for spare parts. He made a good living restoring antique and late model tractors for resale to the gentleman farmers moving into the area who used them for little else other than mowing their oversized lawns. Occasionally, a farmer needing a cheap second tractor with a bucket for snowplowing or moving manure or silage around the farm would buy one of his rebuilt models.

Pete and Art had a long-standing antipathy. Art's father had been hired by the bank to sell off the Trepanier Farm in '42, while Pete was off "fightin' krauts" overseas. He came home to find his parents living in a small tenement house on the Stewart property and working for a pittance for Lyle and Ned as farm help. The farm he grew up on now belonged to an enterprising neighbor who had finally succeeded in buying it to expand his holdings and add the extensive hayfields for additional winter forage to feed his growing herd of milkers.

Inured to violence from his experience in the Ardennes, Pete had to be calmed down by neighbors and friends. He saw the loss of his family's farm and the nooks and crannies of his childhood in the way he imagined French peasants had experienced the arrogance of German occupation: His own parents, now working as tenants for another farmer, his birthplace now an adjunct to a neighbor's farm, and the house he was raised in used as a tenant house for other farmworkers, like his parents. It was all too much for Pete. Had he not been worried about his aging parents, he would have taken off. He spent the next few years drinking too much and working for the local International Harvester dealer, doing implement and tractor repair work. Over the years, however, his anger ebbed and he took a job as a handyman for the newly arrived Union Carbide Corporation, which had built a records storage facility in Morrisville. His anger at Art had by now attenuated to the point of taking any opportunity to take make fun of him.

Pete had his eye on an old Ford 8N tractor coming up for sale right after lunch. He considered the 8N one of the better-engineered tractors to date. He specialized in smaller tractors he could afford like the 8N, Farmall A, or Deere MT. Pete set his maximum price at $45 on the Ford, the engine of which was seized. It also needed new rubber, a paint job, and a radiator.

Much to Pete's annoyance and disgust, a tony stranger in seersucker pants acquired the rusty tractor hulk for $125. Pete took solace in knowing that the stranger's cost of restoration would be considerably more than the tractor's market value. Still, he was annoyed to lose it.

As brown bags mushroomed among the bidders and the sun began its afternoon descent, Lurlene was outside cleaning up the mess customers had made of the condiment table and Frank was shutting down the grill. The deep fat fryer stayed on, as many departing auction-goers would buy a greasy bag of fried dough to take home with them.

Pete watched as a tedder and side rake went for half their used value. As much as he loved machines, ones that lacked internal combustion engines held little interest for him.

After the last implements and large hand tools had all been sold, the audience braced itself for Art's usual banter about the priceless deals available in the odd-lots compiled by Jessica and Maxine in an array of bushel baskets they kept for the purpose. A typical odd-lot was comprised of a mix of hand tools, jars of nails and screws, kitchen knives and silverware, oil cans, pots and pans, light bulbs, books, cleaning products, whisk brooms, dust pans, flower pots, glassware, record albums, framed prints, clocks and the like. Jessica knew to thoroughly mix goods so that one could not bid only for tools or housewares, but would have to make all or nothing bids.

"Okay, everybody, this is the moment we've all been waiting for. This is when the real bargains begin. All odd-lots start at $1.00 and if I don't hear a better bid in 30 seconds, it's yours for a dollar. Now pay attention and let's get to work and remember he or she who hesitates, loses.

"This first lot here is a mix of useful goodies, go to a department store and fill up a box with these items and you'll be looking at $30 minimum. Do I hear a dollar? Don't keep me waiting. Bid now or lose it. I have a dollar; do I hear two? Going... going... three over there on number 17. Do I hear four? Going... going... sold to number 17.

"Next lot, girls. Jessica, here hold it up and pull a few of these treasures up so our bidders can see what they're bidding on. Come on now, steal this lot. Don't make me give it away. Let's go! I hear a one. Do I hear a three? Come on, boy and girls. Don't lose this treasure trove. You'll kick yourselves.

"Who'll gimme three? I got two. Come on, who'll gimme three? Let's go. Three! Gimme four. Four! Gimme five. Five on you. Who'll gimme six? Now, we're movin'. I got six, seven, eight on number 11. Do I hear nine? I got eight on you. This discerning gentlewoman knows quality when she sees it. Nobody else? Let's go. Don't let her steal it from you. Do I hear nine? Come on folks. It's gettin' late. There, I got ten! Let me hear twelve! I got twelve, now fifteen. I got fifteen, Twenty? Give me twenty. Come on boys and girls. I hear twenty. On you with the John Deere shirt at twenty... do I hear $25? 30 on Pete. Now there's someone who understands value. Pete's in the bidding. You know there's money to be made!

"You gonna let Pete have this? Now $35 on Rod Jimmo. Rod, good to have you in the game! Pete you in or out? It's on Rod at $35. $40 on Pete, now $45 on Rod and, whoa, we have a new bidder, Jimmy Bates at $50. 50 on number 16. 55 on Rod and to you Pete. Gimme 60? $60 on Pete. Whoa, what the hell's in that box anyway? They must know something boys. There's something of value in there. Don't let it get away. $70 on Jimmy. 80 on Pete. $100 on Rod. Yes sir, now we're talking."

Art began to look nervous. He grabbed the box away from Maxine and began pawing through it, worried that Maxine and Jessica had missed something valuable. A cursory scan showed the usual collection of junk.

Art began again. "Where were we? Let's see," he said with a nod from Annie, "$100 on Rod, number 36. You all done boys? Do I hear $125? All done...? Jimmy Bates at $125 number 16. Pete, you in or out...? Pete Trepanier at $150, number 20."

Art glanced fretfully at the box that was now sitting in the middle of the platform.

"Boys, you know something I don't? What's hiding in there, damn it? There must be something."

Meanwhile the shouted bids kept up without Art who was now pawing frantically through the box, opening old hard-cover Westerns, reading album jackets, scrutinizing old framed prints, and trying to read the etching on kitchen knives and maker's marks on old nickel-silver forks and spoons.

Annie was keeping track of the bidding, which was now between Pete, Rod, and Jimmy who kept going in $50 increments. Unbeknown to Art, who was frantic to find what made the lot so valuable, the high bid had reached $700. Art picked up the megaphone and asked Annie where the bidding left off. Annie yelled back that it was on number 20, Pete at $700.

"Okay boys, I give up, what in blazes is so damn valuable?"

"You sellin' this lot or you gonna play games. I ain't done biddin'," Pete yelled back at Art.

"Me, neither," shouted Rod.

"I'm still in," added Jimmy.

The crowd cheered with yells of "Yeah! Keep going!"

"Okay boys, we're at $700 on you Pete. Do I hear anyone else?"

"800 ..., 900..., 1000..., 1100..."

The bids climbed quickly between the three men. Each time the bid fell to Rod, he'd scratch the back of his head and ponder until the crowd egged him on and he'd raise his paddle upping the ante another $100.

When the bidding slowed and the three had reached $2600, Art was frantic. He was on his knees and had laid out all the objects on the platform and was scrutinizing them individually, totally ignoring the furious bidding in the background and the cheers of the crowd egging the bidders on.

Finally, a sudden silence in the crowd distracted Art from his frantic searching. He stood up and looked up at the crowd confused. Chuckles started here and there and finally erupted into roars of laughter. Art looked confused. He again yelled to Annie to find out where the bidding stood so he could hammer down a close. Her answer, though, was obscured by the roar of a departing truck with a blown muffler. Art looked up and saw Pete, Rod and Jimmy drive off in Pete's truck with Jimmy standing in the back waving his number 16 paddle at Art and holding up a bottle of Carling's with the other. The crowd cheered and waved at the departing pickup.

Art had Annie send the $2600 bill to Pete with a note saying if he ever planned to drive again, he'd have to pay up and pick up his pricey goods if he wanted his driver's license back.

Pete mailed the bill back with a note scratched on it saying only, "Look at the expiration date on the license, asshole."

Jeeter Buries His Parents

THE ONLY THING Jeeter's mother Selma feared more than being buried alive was not being buried at all. She remembered and often retold to young Jeeter about when Miss Lucas, her fifth grade teacher, made the class read and discuss Poe's *The Fall of the House of Usher*. She focused the class discussion on their thoughts about being buried alive and effectively instilled in her 11-year-old charges her own most deep-seated fear.

Selma bore this terror throughout her long life. In her dotage, Selma's mother had confided to her that their family had a "touch of the tar brush," going back to her own great grandmother who was a slave before the Civil War and, ever since, "women in the family bought burial insurance even though they was mostly white."

Whenever Jeeter mentioned his mother's terror to friends, he explained, "It's generic, runs in our fambly. I heard tell Doctor Phil carries a long hat pin in his med'cine case and pricks it into a dead person's heart to be sure they'se dead."

When Jeeter went to visit his parents in their trailer after two weeks unloading log trucks in Moscow, he found his mother dead on the couch and his father dead drunk in a lawn chair in the front yard. It was cold enough to hang meat and his father, sitting in a moraine of beer cans, looked dead too. When Jeeter addressed him, he said only, "Your mother's dead inside. What'm I gonna do now?"

Jeeter called his friend Clare Reynolds. Clare had been the Overseer of the Poor before "the Welfare" took over. He occasionally helped Jeeter out of scrapes when he was "in 'streamus." This was Jeeter's hearing of Clare's term "in extremis."

"I'se in streamus," Jeeter yelled into his neighbor's four-party line when he finally got through to Clare. "Ma's dead and Pa's wishin' he was.... need'dja to come up right away."

"Take it easy, Jeeter, I'll be up with Doctor Phil. He's the Lamoille County Medical Examiner and he'll have to pronounce your Ma dead and he'll take a look at your Pa. He's probably just had a shock."

"And half case 'a beer," Jeeter muttered into the receiver.

"I thought your parents didn't drink," said Clare.

"They don't," answered Jeeter.

"Lucky genetics runs down generations, not up," said Clare.

"What's generics have to do with Pa dying?"

"Nothing, Jeeter, forget it. Now, stay outta the screech 'til I get there. Ya hear?"

Jeeter hung up. He hadn't thought much about screech, since he'd left his own trailer to go down to Moscow to work the lumber trucks at Adams. They didn't allow any drinking in the lumberyard so Jeeter left his stash of pints at home. If you showed up drunk or even sporting a hangover, you were fired, your name was put on a list and you'd never be hired again. This limited the lumber company's labor force considerably in Lamoille County.

Jeeter was trying to talk to his father when Clare's pickup rolled into the yard with Dr. Phil in the passenger seat. There was no driveway since Jeeter's parents had no car and relied on their son to drive them to town once a week to trade or to go to the doctor if the need arose.

"Your dad'll be fine when he sobers up. Don't believe I've ever seen him drunk before. Where'd he get the beer? You been down to Moscow workin' lumber I heard," Dr. Phil added.

"Dad must 'a walked over ta Floyd's when Mom got sick. You know Floyd... b'lieves beer cures ever'thing, even death. He probably got Pa drunk and sent him home with a case for hisself...can't remember if I ever saw Dad 'toxicated... he ain't never been a drinker and Ma's a teetotaler."

Jeeter followed Clare and Dr. Phil into the trailer. His mother lay on the trailer's built-in bench-couch. On her chest lay an official paper that Jeeter hadn't noticed before. Dr. Phil picked it up and began reading.

"Well, I'll be goddamned. Ha'n't see one of these in twenty years. Your mom bought burial insurance. Must 'a been afraid you had a shovel," he snickered.

"Ain't funny, Doc, she's my kin," muttered Jeeter, hurt by the implication.

All I need to do is call this here number and mail a death certificate and they'll send through a check that'll cover funeral and burial costs."

"How much?" Jeeter asked.

"Up to $3500," answered Dr. Phil.

"Christ, I could buy a new truck with that."

"You aren't buyin' no new truck with your mother's burial insurance. This is her money. She paid for it and we're gonna use it to bury her proper the way she wanted to be. She didn't want to burden you with her burial costs. Y'ought 'a be grateful instead of resenting. I'll call Black's Funeral Home and they'll take care of the whole thing. If there is any left over, it gets dispersed according to her will. I suspect you'll get it since you don't have any brothers or sisters to fight over it with and she wasn't a church lady."

"They got discounts at Black's? She's a small woman."

"This isn't up to you, Jeeter. Respect your mother's wishes and stay out of it. Don't go pikering Jack Black. He'll do right by your Ma in her last moments on this earth. That's what she wanted."

"I s'pose," muttered Jeeter.

Dr. Phil and Clare carried Selma out to the truck while Jeeter stood by rubbing his chapped hands together and watched as Clare and Dr. Phil backed out of the driveway with Selma between them. His father had resumed snoring in his lawn chair. Jeeter went into the house to fortify himself with some screech and to fetch a wool blanket to cover his father who was looking increasingly ashen.

As he collapsed into his father's recliner to have a pull from his pint, he heard Clare's truck pull back into the yard. Jeeter hid the pint under the recliner and dashed out into the yard.

"What's up, Ma better?" he said as the engine died.

"No, she's still dead, Jeeter. She ain't coming back."

"Dj'ou stick that hat pin in her heart like you'se s'posed ta, Doc?"

"Jeeter, what are you talking about?"

"I heard tell you keep a hat pin for testing if the dead's really dead."

"Jeeter, that's nonsense. Listen, did your ma have false teeth?"

"Yes, I b'lieve so. Why ya askin'? Need some?"

"Jeeter, I don't need false teeth... yet... certainly not your mother's, but Jack will if he's ta make her up nice for the viewing. Now, run in and fetch 'em. I want to get over to Jack's 'cause I don't know how long she's been lying on that bench."

Jeeter ran back into the front yard clutching a set of false teeth.

"Here they are, right on her bedstead where she puts 'em ever' night 'fore she goes to sleep."

"Thanks," Clare said, pocketing the teeth and getting back in the truck.

Jeeter watched Doc and Clare drive off with his mother and then returned to a stiff pull of screech.

He soon drifted off into a twitchy sleep, only to wake a few hours later. The sun was setting and a damp fall cold was settling over the valley. His father, too, had drifted off and Jeeter set about trying to wake him up and bring him into the trailer where the small, brown enamel stove in the corner, with its inverted glass bottle of kerosene feeding it, warmed the trailer. Jeeter's dad had recovered from his hangover, but still did not look well. As Jeeter laid him out on the couch near the stove where he had found his mother that morning, he covered him with a patchwork quilt from their bedroom in the back of the trailer. He heard his father whisper, "What'd they do with my Selma?"

"Clare and Dr. Phil took her to the funeral home to get buried," Jeeter answered.

"Ma had burial insurance," his father again whispered.

"I know, Clare's gonna see to it that she gets buried proper and 'ss all paid for. I'll stay here with you tonight, but I've to git home tomorrow to feed Rooter. He ain't much long for this world either with his 'splasia. Draggin' his hind legs again, must 'a got worse when the weather turned. I've to help him into the trailer by liftin' his hind quarters. You get some sleep now, Pa. I'll see you in the morning."

*   *   *

The following morning, Jeeter couldn't rouse his father.

Jeeter plucked a piece of down sticking out of the quilt he'd put over him the night before and set it under his father's nose to see if he was breathing, but the down didn't move.

"Dad!" Jeeter yelled, "Wake up! It's mornin' time."

But there was no response from the inert body lying on the couch.

Clare and Dr. Phil showed up about half hour later in Clare's pickup.

"Damned if what they say ain't true," Clare observed, looking at Jeeter's father. "A couple married as long as they been dies within days 'a each other. Poor Elmer only waited one."

"Elmer have burial insurance, too?" Dr. Phil asked Jeeter.

"He din't b'lieve in it," said Jeeter, wiping tears away with a greasy blue handkerchief he plucked from the front of his bib overalls.

"Can't believe Pa's gone, too ... don't seem right ...must 'a missed Ma terrible. He 'as a good man, self defecatin'. Shat on hisself even though others respected 'im."

The next day, after Clare and Dr. Phil had taken Jeeter's father to Copley Hospital to determine the cause of death and complete the death certificate, Jeeter walked in and asked what he should do next. Selma was embalmed and laid out in a modest casket chosen by the funeral director to match the check they would receive from the burial insurance company.

"What'm I gonna do with Dad? He din't b'lieve in burial insurance and I ain't got the money to lay him ta rest. What'm I to do naow? Maybe the funeral people'll have a casket that'd fit two?"

"Jeeter, it's much cheaper to cremate. You could have Elmer cremated," Clare suggested.

"Like I did the woodshed siding?" Jeeter asked.

"What are you talking about, the woodshed? You thinkin' on cremat-in' him yourself... if so, you're nuts. 'Sides, it's illegal. What are you talking about?" Clare said, raising his voice to Jeeter, who again looked hurt. "You been in the screech again. It's mornin' for Chrissake."

"No, I ain't been drinkin'. What'choo think 'a me anyway?" Jeeter said, looking even more hurt.

"I cremosoted the shed last year so it woon't rot away like the shitter did. Hardware guy said it'd keep it from rottin' and it worked. Din't know they used cremosote to preserve people, too. I can see how it'd work bet-ter'n 'bombing 'em."

"Jesus, Jeeter, I'm talking about cremation where you take the body to a crematorium and they burn the body down to a few ashes that you can sprinkle over his land or bury with Selma. It's cheaper than a cas-ket and burial. They just use a cardboard coffin. Whole thing cost about $250 bucks. I can have Jack come over with his hearse and drive Elmer to the crematorium."

"What's 'at cost?"

"Maybe Jack'd do it for fifty bucks. It's up in St. J."

"If, you'd jess tell me where the creamery is, I'd take him there myself in the pickup... ain't that far."

"Jeeter, it's illegal to transport a corpse yourself... State laws against it. 'Sides it's a crematory. Creamery's where they bottle milk."

"You and Dr. Phil done it."

"Selma wasn't declared dead yet. It was an emergency trip. That's legal."

"We both know'd she's dead. So 'at's why Dr. Phil din't use the hatpin, 'cause he'd get in trouble for transportin' a crops."

"Jeeter, you've been drinking."

"Just poured a little bit in my coffee. What's so bad in that?"

"Oh, Jesus, did you remember to put in any coffee?"

Clare arranged for the funeral home to transport Elmer to the crematorium in St. Johnsbury for money he had already received from Selma's insurance. Dr. Phil and Clare split the cost of the crematory services with an understanding that Jeeter would pay them back when he sold his parent's trailer and plot.

Jeeter went home to drown his sorrows and to help Rooter, his husky, into the trailer where they shared Milk-Bone dog biscuits for supper. There weren't many year-round residents in Hardwood Flats, so the few neighbors who did hear Jeeter and Rooter howling at a waning moon that night chalked it up to the well known effects of screech on those who drank it.

Selma and Elmer were buried together in Plains Cemetery in Hardwood Flats. Clare and Dr. Phil saw to it that Jeeter was sober for his parents' burial.

After Selma's casket was lowered into the ground, however, Jeeter leaned over the freshly dug grave to pour his father's ashes on top of her, but the gravelly grave edge on which he was standing gave way and he slid feet-first onto the coffin with a loud thud. Clare leaned down and helped him scramble out. Clare noticed the powerful smell of screech and shook his head as the few mourners tried to suppress their smiles. Dusting the dirt and his mother's ashes off the dark suit he'd borrowed from Clare, Jeeter muttered to the few assembled, "They mussa wanted me to come with 'em, but I ain't ready yet, sides can't afford it."

Mr. Leonard's Two-holer

MR. LEONARD TAUGHT well before self-esteem became part of the school curriculum. He was a quiet man both in school with his classes of junior high English students and at home with his wife Millie, his spinster daughter, Eva, and his collie, Orwell. Before speaking, he would focus from behind a thicket of anarchic eyebrows and, once you were in his gaze, he'd parse his few words slowly and softly. The chainsaw, tractor, and stockcar boys had to listen carefully when he spoke. Whether helping his charges visualize English grammar by diagramming sentences on a blackboard or guiding them through the narrative mysteries of Eudora Welty and Saki, Mr. Leonard was parsimonious with words, not one to hold forth but rather to come to know and guide his students through their lessons.

With their plentiful siblings, two of his students, Percy Denton and Al Courchaine, worked their parents' neighboring dairy farms. To hear and be heard over the din of compressors, tractors, generators, and chain saws, farm families were accustomed to yelling at one another, even in the absence of engine noises. A loud and practical exchange of views about the day's events and the following day's tasks during supper in the warm farm kitchens was then mimicked as tanned arms crossed each other, reaching across the oak tabletop for ironstone platters filled with buttered turnips, slabs of brown beef steeped in gravy and fall green beans. Their raucous childhoods hardly prepared Percy and Al for Mr. Leonard's subdued classroom, at least until they discovered his canny sense of humor.

When young Leonard arrived in Vermont fresh from the Pacific Theater where he had fought "Japs" in the dank jungles of Borneo, he met Millie. They soon joined the many couples seeking intimacy and security in marriage after the chaos of war. As a wedding gift, Millie's father gave them his modest wood-frame camp on Little Hosmer Pond. Millie was dismayed to learn that the camp would be in the family for yet another generation. As a young girl, Millie grew up dreading the camp's perpetually damp and musty interior, the troops of brazen mice that skittered through the kitchen drawers and along shelves, the mosquitoes buzzing relentlessly at dusk, and the porcupines gnawing away at the board and batten exterior to savor the salty stain. She recalled the misery of crawling into damp linen sheets as a child after a day of clearing brush, forcing a dull hand-mower through overgrown grass, or fishing for slimy bullpout in the pond's murky depths. She reserved her worst fear, however, for peeing in the middle of the night, following the narrow path into the white birch thicket in her nightgown with a flickering lantern to the spider-haunted outhouse. A fan of Jane Austen, Millie found relief in the stark contrast between her father's "camp" and Emma's Hartfield since it meant that warm and elegant places existed somewhere.

Both Percy and Al worked hard in Mr. Leonard's class, learning to ask questions about the unfamiliar tools of grammar — adverbs, adjectives, gerunds, and participles. They both took eagerly to Mr. Leonard's choice of short stories. This trust soon led them to the longer novels he recommended. After reading several books by Jack London and Ernest Thompson Seton, Percy and Al began to regularly ask Mr. Leonard for more suggestions they then found at the small Carnegie Library in Morrisville. In time, they stopped checking the number of pages as their criterion for reading choices.

Mr. Leonard remained a mystery to townspeople. After the war, he and Millie settled in and bought a modest, pale yellow, two-story house, shaded like all the houses on Elmore Street by vast elms. The single-story post-war raised ranches and Flanders Wonder Homes, designed for affordability more than comfort, were just beginning to bloom on the outskirts of town.

Mr. Leonard landed the high school teaching job vacated by Ezra Styles who suffered a stroke while lecturing a rowdy crew of boys and a flirtation of girls over-anxious to become women. Deafness and thick glasses had facilitated Mr. Styles' lectures, as he neither heard nor saw any of the desk-to-desk banter, the jokes about his ill-fitting clothes, or the plotting of sylvan trysts after school. Like background static his lectures on various arcane English writers provided a continuo for an active classroom social life.

After two years, Mr. Leonard asked to be reassigned to junior high where he hoped to inspire a love of learning earlier and perhaps broaden the horizons of those rushing headlong into the working class. His request was answered when he was assigned to seventh grade English to replace Mrs. Dilworth, who disappeared in the middle of the school year amid rumors of her being with child, but without husband.

Mr. Leonard paid attention to all of his students, taking pride in their small successes. The junior high girls seemed to show an easy affinity for the complexities of grammar and the mysteries of the subjunctive tense. He also introduced them to the Brontes, Thomas Hardy, and Jane Austen. The boys who had managed to master reading in the earlier grades, eagerly consumed short stories of action and adventure. Mr. Leonard kept a spiral-bound notebook in which he listed the types of books and the reading levels of each of his students along with a list of titles he could recommend, and he would check them off as they moved through their reading list.

When both Percy and Al submitted their final essays on Mr. Leonard's assigned question on Charles Dickens' "Tale of Two Cities," which Al preferred to call "The Sale of Two Titties" to his friend Percy, Mr. Leonard was so cheered by their depth of understanding that he asked them if they would like to spend a Friday night at his camp and promised to teach the two of them how to fly fish Saturday morning.

Welcoming a day off from the tedium of farm work, Percy and Al accepted and came to school that Friday prepared to leave after school in Mr. Leonard's '54 Ford station wagon for an overnight and a day of fishing at his camp. Mrs. Leonard had filled the back with groceries as she knew the appetites of young boys.

"No need for worms where we're going," said Mr. Leonard with a smile. "I brought an extra fly rod I borrowed from Rod Culver and I've another at the camp that I bought for Millie, but she never took much to fly fishing."

After bouncing several miles down a two-track road through a thicket of hemlocks and blackberry bushes, the road opened out onto a small lawn that sloped down to the shoreline of Little Hosmer. Al and Percy could see a dock with a wooden rowboat lying upside down on it. The camp was sided with board and batten, and had a small deck off the front just roomy enough for two wooden rockers.

The shutters were open and the first thing Millie did after she helped the men bring in the groceries and extra blankets was to open all the windows. Mr. Leonard enlisted the boys help with several armloads of dry ash logs and kindling from a nearby lean-to. Millie removed the butcher paper from eight thick-cut pork chops she'd brought for dinner and wrapped six baking potatoes in tinfoil after slicing them in half and inserting a large pat of butter. She then enlisted Percy to help her shell the peck of fresh peas she'd picked that afternoon from their garden.

After dinner, Mr. Leonard fed the fire and the brisk flame-up kept evening mosquitoes at bay. As the moon rose, Al pointed out the hundreds of bats and purple martins circling low over the pond feeding on insects and dragon-flies while Millie sliced a blueberry pie she'd made that afternoon and dished it out to "the boys," as she called them.

When the dishes were washed and left on the plywood counter to dry, Mr. Leonard and Millie retired but invited the Al and Percy to hang out by the fire if they wished but admonished them not to stay up too late, as they would head off for a day's fishing right after breakfast.

When the lights went out in the master bedroom on the first floor of the camp, Percy reached into his duffle and pulled out two quarts of Carling's Black Label beer. The two lay back and talked quietly into the evening about tractors, their favorite Saki short story, *The Interlopers*, and the girls moving in and out of their lives. They retired to the loft about 11:30 and soon fell fast asleep.

About 3:30 Percy's bladder woke him up. Blinking himself into semi-consciousness, he remembered where he was. He lay there for a few minutes staring at the ceiling rafters and tried to convince himself that he didn't have to go to the bathroom. He finally succumbed, rose quietly from the wood- frame cot, and tiptoed through the moonlight into the living room. He had no intent of making the trek to the outhouse and, like most country boys, knew he could simply pee unseen off the porch at this time of night. But as he slipped out into the three-quarter moon, he began to feel a commensurate pressure building in his bowels and realized he had no choice but to use the outhouse.

Reluctantly, he returned to the sitting room to find the brass Aladdin lantern Mr. Leonard kept on the dining room table handy for such evening trips. Annoyed that Mr. Leonard's sense of adventure precluded a simple flashlight, he fussed with the lantern pump and several matches until he finally got the fragile mantle to emit a white light in the living room. To avoid the squeaks he had noticed earlier from the screen door, he opened and closed it slowly and stepped out into the silver light. He retraced the path Mr. Leonard had shown them for about 20 yards where he found a small outhouse with the classic quarter moon cutout in the wooden door. Had he thought to keep the door open while he relieved himself, he probably could have avoided all the fuss trying to get the complex lantern lit as the moon shone brightly over the pond. Percy was familiar with kerosene lanterns and their simple cotton wicks but this was his first experience with a mantle lantern.

As he opened the door, the lantern sputtered and went out. He realized he hadn't kept the pressure pumped up. Rather than go back and get more matches, Percy decided simply to leave the door open hoping for enough light to see the interior.

It was very dark inside but a mother-of-pearl toilet seat fastened to the wooden bench reflected just enough moonlight so Percy knew where to sit down. Seated, he set the lantern down next to him on the bench only to hear a loud plop. Panicked, he looked to his right and in the shadows realized the outhouse was a two-holer and that he had dropped the lantern into the adjacent hole.

This was not like dropping a flashlight that could be replaced for $2.00 and Percy panicked. Annoyed that the lantern had failed and that he had not been unable to see and recognize a two-holer, he was grateful that the lantern was not glowing at some precarious angle in the mound of stools beneath. He'd heard of kerosene lanterns igniting methane gas.

After seeing to his own needs, he began to think about how to recover Mr. Leonard's brass lantern. From the "plop," it seemed that it was not that far down below the rim of the bench.

Percy wiped himself with damp toilet paper on a dowel hanging from the wall, the edges of which had been nibbled by mice making nesting materials, and ran back to the house. He removed a candle from the brass candelabrum on the fold-down desk, grabbed the box of kitchen matches and ran back to the outhouse. He lit the candle and lowered it as far down as he could reach below the bench seat. The lantern was about five feet below the hole, too far for him to reach. He would need a hook of some sort.

He tipped the candle sideways and dripped some wax onto the bench seat beside the one he had used and set the candle in it firmly. He then went back to the house to search for a tool to fish out the brass lantern. The first object to catch his eye was Mr. Leonard's bamboo fly rod hanging on two nails in the wall over the dining room table. The length would certainly reach deep enough, but how would he hook the lantern's bale so he could pull it up through the hole? There was a tiny May fly on the end of the pole but the hook looked too small to catch on the brass bale.

After searching silently everywhere but in the bedroom occupied by Mr. and Mrs. Leonard, he finally found an old steel bait-casting rod and reel in the tool closet. It had a number ten hook on it, big enough to hold a generous knot of night crawlers.

Percy tiptoed out of the cabin and ran back to the outhouse. The candle still glowed on the edge of the adjacent seat. Percy pulled some line from the reel. The noise of the reel's detent surprised him in the silent evening. He then poked the end of the fish pole into the hole and shifted it around in an effort to snag the lantern's bale that had fallen to the side.

After several vain attempts, he finally snagged it and drew the befouled lantern up through the hole. He did not set it down, but blew out the candle, grabbed the rod and reel, and left the outhouse, forgetting to sprinkle the enamel cup's worth of wood ash onto his fresh deposit.

Percy found his way to the lakeshore where he carefully rinsed the bottom of the lantern off, reset the fish hook into the cork lining handle behind the reel and walked slowly back to the camp. On the way back to the cottage he could see streaks of red light on the eastern horizon.

He replaced the rod on the wall and set the lantern on the table where he found it and replaced the candle in its holder on the desk.

Finally back on his cot, he heard Al mutter something in his sleep and then resume a gently snore. It took a half-hour for the adrenalin to leach out of Percy's system and for him to fall back asleep.

The smell of coffee and bacon woke them both. They dressed hastily and went into the main room where Mr. Leonard was nursing a coffee and Millie was setting out enamelware dishes.

"Catch anything last night?" Mr. Leonard asked Percy.

The Invisible Fence

"SIX KIDS IN all, but I only bred four of 'em. Other two's steps. Came with my new wife, Gert. First wife, Sal, leff me couple years ago. Said I'd out-lived my pecker, but it came back to life when I met Gert, as she likes to tell," Wyvis announced in answer to Doc Chapin's question about his family. "Now, where's you thinkin' of puttin' this 'ere fence?"

"All around the property... there's boundary marking pipes sticking out of the four corners. It's about two acres. I can show you where they are. I'd like the fence to follow those lines. Our dog, Loomis, got into Millie Sanders' ducks and she's apoplectic about it."

"Oh, a bible-thumper, eh?"

"Huh?

"So what kind fence you want: post 'n rail, barb wire, chicken wire, 'lectric? I do all kinds."

"It's in that box over there. It's one of them new invisible fences."

"Invisible, then what'cha need me for if'n iss invisible? Some kin' a joke? Sure you din't get snookered, bein' new in these parts 'n all?"

"No, I had one down where I used to live in New Haven. They're great for keeping your dog near home. If the dog goes near the buried fence, a signal goes off and his collar sends him a shock to know to stay away. Works like a champ."

"So, it's like an unnerground 'lectric fence?"

"Exactly, I've already gotten off on a bad foot with Millie and I want to make it up to her."

"She's a misogynist I hear tell. Ain't never had one 'a 'em in town afore."

"Women can't be misogynists, only men can be misogynists."

"No, she is one. I had to look it up from her sign out front. Charges $35 an hour... b'lieve it? I dig fence and only charge $12. I should go into mysoging."

"She's masseuse, she gives massages. They're good for you, reduce stress and relax you. You should try it some time. A misogynist is a woman-hater."

"I was one 'a 'em once when I's married to Sal, Glad she left... drank all my beer and then some... used to beat on me when she's drunk, too.

Massages is where she rubs you all down naked, right? $35 don't sound so bad for that deal. I'd say. Sounds like a good deal, if'n y'ask me. Might try one. She pretty?"

"It isn't like that, Wyvis. She massages your muscles and then you relax."

"All my muscles?"

"Not that one, and besides, that isn't a muscle. It's an inflatable."

"Sometimes mine don't inflate, need a bicycle pump, I s'pose."

"Can we just talk about the fence?"

"Hard to if'n it's invisible."

XXXX

When Jilly and Betty gave up farming after 37 years and moved in with their son Will, one Jack Bauer from Montclair, New Jersey bought their 42-acres with the idea of restoring and living in the farmhouse and developing the easterly field into Craftsbury's first planned development of 14 two-acre lots. There were no zoning laws in Craftsbury to contend with, only feisty neighbors. The only town zoning, in the form of an unspoken understanding, was that if you lived on The Green, you could paint your house any color you wanted, as long as it was white.

Jack marketed the plots in his home state and sold seven lots handily to people looking to retire in a rural setting. The small development had a common green with a cattail-snapping turtle-duckweed pond in the center with three wooden benches for enduring the mosquitoes breeding in the pond and the baritone chorus of bullfrogs that began practice at dusk. Dogs were allowed as long as there were no complaints.

A Neighborhood Development Committee, composed of volunteer residents was given the power to pre-approve exterior building design and color, any outbuildings like garden sheds or detached garages, lawn paraphernalia such as gym sets, follies, compost heaps, vegetable plots, swimming pools, barbecue set-ups, and fencing. Clotheslines and drying racks were considered déclassé and were forbidden, as were external combustion engines except family automobiles and lawn mowers. Mowing was restricted to Thursdays and Saturdays between 9 A.M. and 5 P.M. Each home was limited to ownership of two functioning vehicles, only one of which could be parked outside overnight.

These restrictions were a source of endless amusement to locals, for whom property ownership conveyed unrestricted rights. The idea that one could not leave clothes to dry in the sun, have a half-dozen parts-cars on the lawn, or fence in a few chickens or a pig was absurd. Locals marveled at the constraints that down-country buyers put up with, especially given the inflated prices they paid for their two-acre plots. As Marc Lavoie was overheard to say one night in Mer-Lu's while some locals were making fun of the development, "Ya jess know, the man or woman who really wants to be on that committee what decides what you can do with your prop'ty is the person you really don' want there." Several heads nodded in agreement.

Doc Chapin and his wife, Sarah, were one of the earlier buyers. Doc retired from a hospital in New Haven where for 22 years on the evening shift, he treated a never-ending succession of gunshot and knife wounds, children with asthma, seniors with dementia, overweight people with diabetic emergencies, and drug and alcohol accidents, then returning home midnight. With his wife Sarah's assent, he resigned and the two planned their move to Vermont. He was soon offered a job in the nearby Copley Hospital in Morrisville and took the job after a single interview. He and Sarah, a former executive assistant in a New Haven law firm, loved their new home. Their first purchase was a small Jotul gas stove for the living room, complete with fake logs visible through its glass door. Claire Couture oversaw the social services at the hospital and was often called upon to contend with pets orphaned by their owner's death. She convinced Doc Chapin to adopt a scatty golden retriever named Loomis, whose former owner's last request was to ask Claire "to see to my dog, Loomis, and find him a kindly owner," before she succumbed to emphysema. After consulting with his wife Sarah, he brought the seven-year-old Loomis home.

Loomis was eager and friendly but liked to roam and had little patience for fowl or feline. He was used to having free rein. After the death of three of Millie's ducks in a down-filled killing spree, it was clear Loomis needed to be fenced in. Doc Chapin mail-ordered an invisible fence and, after inquiring about someone to install it, he met Wyvis.

To his surprise, Doc found the fence would require an application and pre-approval by the Development Committee before he could engage Wyvis to install it. The form required a written rationale for the fence as well as a description of what the fence would look like when finished. The form had to be submitted with before and after photographs of the area to be fenced in. The directions explained that the "after" photo could be an artist's rendering or a marketing image from the fence provider.

Doc and Sarah were flummoxed. They filled out the form as best they could and submitted it without any pictures, explaining that the fence was invisible. The form came back stamped "INCOMPLETE SUBMISSION."

They looked over the form carefully to see what they had missed. Every question had been answered truthfully. It was clear from their answers that the fence was to be underground and would be buried along the lot's perimeter. Sarah took pains to write out the installation process and then her husband suggested they include a copy of the instructions. The next day at work, he made a copy and then resubmitted the application, stapled to a copy of the elaborate instructions for installing the fence. The entire form came back the following day again stamped "INCOMPLETE SUBMISSION.

The couple's confusion shifted to frustration and anger.

"The locals may have a point," fumed Doc. "This is ridiculous. I can live with the restrictions we signed on to, but what do they want from us? No one'll ever even see this fence."

Sarah agreed to go the Development Committee meeting the following Wednesday and petition for approval in person or to find out what was missing from their application. That night both husband and wife got home late and met over a glass of wine.

"So.... How'd it go? Were you able to find out what their problem is?"

"You won't believe it. Mrs. Desmond is the chair of the committee. She started out by lecturing me about how important it is to follow rules... Imagine, lecturing me, who worked for 18 years for a type-A law partner! I asked her politely what rule we had failed to follow. She said, 'You failed to include the before and after photographs,' to which I indicated there wouldn't be any difference.

She then started in, 'Rules have a purpose. They are an organizing principle of...' at which point I walked out, unwilling to hear the rest of her self-righteous crap. What a bitch! I agree with the locals. Let's buy a house somewhere else. We can bring our Jotul and Loomis."

"Calm down, Honey. You've every right to be upset. I've got an idea."

"I hope it doesn't involving caving into that bitch."

The next day Doc Chapin took two identical Polaroid pictures of their lot. With a magic marker he marked one "before" and the other "after," clipped them to the already substantial application and dropped it off at the development office on his way to work.

The following week the application came back, stamped "APPROVED."

Doc called Wyvis and told him he had approval to start the fence project. He also made the mistake of telling Wyvis the story of their efforts to get it approved.

Several weeks later, Doc was about to remove Neal Hoadley's appendix when his chief surgical nurse handed him the required patient liability waiver, to which was attached a before and after shot of Neal's naked beer belly. It took Doc a minute to get the joke.

Dog Camp

ART LOST HIS Mansfield ski patrol job for a prank greatly enjoyed by his ski patrol buddies. Although the injured Montreal doctor strapped to a toboggan yelling his lungs out about all the people he was going to sue as Art headed down the fall-line of the Nose Dive at full speed with the toboggan between his legs sounded less amused.

Art was a terrific skier and managed to keep the careening sled in control until he went airborne off the jump on the Nose Dive's run-out. He later asserted in a vain self-defense before being fired, that he thought the ride might stimulate the injured doctor's blood pressure before he arrived in the emergency room to have the compound fracture in his right leg set.

During the jump, the heavy fiberglass toboggan followed its own trajectory and shot forward through Art's legs yanking the safety harness free and peeling Art's gloves from his hands. The immobilized doctor was now soloing.

The sled touched ground thirty feet beyond the jump, landing nose first and cart-wheeling end-over-end several times on the trail before coming to rest upside down in deep powder along the trail's edge. As Art christied up to the inverted sled, he could still hear the muffled oaths and threats emanating from under the sled and snow.

Art turned over the sled, brushed some snow from his patient's face, and again tried to calm him but to no avail. He knew he'd overstepped this time. The doctor spluttered half in Canuck and half in English about pain and suffering, personal assault, and a massive settlement as Art snowplowed off slowly to the ambulance waiting at the bottom of the mountain.

His colleague Jess helped him "board" the still fulminating patient, whose leg Art had splinted on the trail, and the two hefted the doctor into the ambulance. Art's boss came running onto the scene and, showing no amusement, fired Art on the spot. Jess tapped the ambulance twice, the signal to depart and the ambulance sped off with its siren wailing.

Distracted as he listened to yet another angry person yelling at him, Art had not closed the ambulance door, and as the ambulance drove through the base lodge parking lot, the folded gurney holding the doctor slid out with a loud clatter onto the frozen gravel, launching renewed threats and bilingual invective.

Art knew not to wait around for his final check. He threw his skis over his shoulder and headed for his pickup, contemplating his new unemployment.

Sally was used to Art's short-term employment stints and as a backstop had opened her own business on the farm they rented in nearby Moscow. Sally loved dogs and before she married Art had worked at an animal shelter as a veterinary assistant. She had always dreamed of making a living doing what she loved and so started Sally's Dog Camp, a day camp for the fancy pooches of Stowe. Dog Camp usually had five to ten canine tenants, a manageable number for Sally and now, Art. There were no kennels at Dog Camp. Guests were free to roam the property, explore, run, and chase wildlife. They were all coaxed with kibble into the barn, or house if it was bitter cold, when night fell.

A week before Thanksgiving, Sally got a call from her former employer asking if she would adopt a dog herself. There was no more information, just that Clarence Tatro had died down near Samoset and his youngest son, Herald, who was 72, "din't want no wild hound to feed," adding that he could barely feed himself. Sally agreed, thinking no more about it. Three days later she was refilling the watering buckets for her thirteen guests and heard a large truck winding up the dirt road to Dog Camp. She watched the truck approach and was surprised to see some kind of shelter on the truck bed. As the truck rounded the house and pulled into the yard, it became evident that the shelter was a dog house and chained to it was a large hound looking curiously at the proceedings.

The truck lurched to a stop and the driver killed the motor.

"I'se Herald, Clarence's boy," the grizzled man said. "Where's your man?"

Sally looked from the dog to the man and answered that Art was at the feed store buying kibble for the dogs.

"You muss be rich ta 'ford that stuff. Bear, here, eats mostly leftovers and venison parts. 'Casionally, I shoot 'im a coon. He's vicious don' cha know. He'll bite th'hand what feeds 'im. Bit Pa so's he bled once... vicious bastard. If you'd n't a took 'im. I'd a shot 'im and buried 'im. Got a tractor with a bucket? Can't unhook 'im from the doghouse, he'll either bite cha wicked or runaway. We can unload him and the doghouse with the tractor. He's been chained ta that house since Pa'd his stroke and stopped hunting two years back. You don' ever wanna unhook 'im."

Sally went over to the shed and started up the International. She drove it over and leveled the bucket against the truck's flatbed.

"Go'in. G'wan in, Bear. Bear'll go in if'in ya tell 'im nice."

Bear disappeared into the doghouse. Clarence clambered up onto the flatbed and pushed the doghouse sideways onto the bucket. Sally raised the bucket and dog-house slightly and backed away, setting the doghouse on the ground near the shed. Still curious, Bear watched from the inside with his face peering out through the doorway.

Sally walked over to Bear.

"I'se warnin' ya, don cha go near 'im. He'll bite cha wicked."

Sally held out her hand. Bear sniffed it and she unbuckled the nylon collar. Bear looked around and bounded off behind the barn.

"Bi-i-ig mistake, you prob'em now'cha unhitched 'im," Herald said, shaking his head and climbing into the cab of the truck.

Sally yelled a "thank you" over the motor and watched as the truck raised a mist of snow as it drove off down the road.

Sally went back in the house to make a cup of coffee and noticed Bear sitting upright on the couch watching intently the Channel Three weather report. She sat down next to him and scratched him gently behind the ears, but he was not to be distracted.

Art came in just as the news started.

"Jesus, you know he's a Bluetick, the real thing, beautiful animal and very sweet."

"Jesus nothing, $40 bucks worth of dog food... I bet you don't spend that much at Patch's on our food!" Art laughed.

"Ya, but I don't buy 200 pounds at a clip. Besides, those folks pay dearly for our care and feeding of their hounds while they're flapping their gums and sucking down rum in Barbados."

Art popped two Narragansetts, plopped down on the couch and, together, the three watched the evening news, Bear looking up at Sally only when she stopped scratching his ears and nape.

"Seems right at home," said Art.

"Ours now, aren't 'cha Bear."

That night the temperature was projected to drop into the teens and Sally suggested that the dogs spend the night inside. "Everyone seems to get along and there's plenty of space," she added.

"Fine by me," said Art.

"Those used mattresses we got free from the Round Hearth work great and I covered most of 'em with tarps so's they don't get groaty and harbor cooties."

"You and your cooties!"

That Sunday, Sally's mother was joining them for an early Sunday dinner. Tessie was a Philadelphia Biddle and had a summer place in Greensboro. Although she had her doubts about her son-in-law's intermittent careers as a ski patrolman, roofer, singer-songwriter, and maple syrup magnate, she loved him and understood better than her social peers her daughter and son-in-law's deep love of life in Vermont. That same love had brought her grandfather to Vermont at the turn of the century and drew him back every year until he retired on the shores of Caspian Lake.

Art heard the Volvo wagon pull up and park near the front porch. He and Sally had seen to it that the dogs were all outdoors. A light snowfall the night before had refinished the landscape and the ramshackle farm, burying the various chew toys, bones, and garbage wrested from the dumpster by a boxer and a Jack Russell, both now returned home.

Mrs. Biddle walked carefully up the bluestone steps onto the rickety porch. Sally opened the door and greeted her mother with a kiss and a hug.

"Where's the furry welcoming committee?" her mother asked.

"Oh, they're out enjoying the new snow," Sally answered.

"It smells wonderful in here. Is that bacon I smell?

"Yes, we're having uncured bacon from the pig we bought next door and fresh eggs from the biddies in the barn. Art installed more chicken wire. The girls are feeling more secure now that the rampaging raccoon that was decimating their flock can't get in. They're back laying full time. Art added some daylights and a timer and that doubled production. They think it's summer even though the sun sets at 4:30."

Art, Sally and Mrs. Biddle sat down at the oval oak dining table. Sally had ironed and spread a hand-embroidered white linen table cloth that Tessie Biddle remembered from her childhood. An arrangement of dried wheat stalks, garlic scapes, and cattail fronds stood in a Mason jar in the middle of the table flanked by jelly jars of wild blueberry and wild blackberry jams that Sally had put up in late summer.

Art drained the bacon and brought it to the table along with a platter of scrambled eggs. Art's mother had taught him how to scramble eggs and Sally always let him prepare them. Art separated the yolks and whites and whipped them separately. He then added the yolks to the butter sizzling in the cast iron pan and when they began to stiffen, added the whipped whites, giving the mixture the consistency of melted cheese and bringing out the rich flavor of the bright yellow yolks.

Sally brought a tray of corn muffins from the oven and the three sat down in front of the picture window overlooking the valley to enjoy breakfast. Each fall, Art set mulch-hay bales around the perimeter of the old farmhouse to reduce the drafts that blew in between the warped sills and the dry-laid stone foundation. This made it possible for their old Defiant woodstove to heat the first and second floors to a comfortable temperature.

The rich smells from the kitchen soon attracted the paying guests, however, and they began competing for a perch on the hay bales below the picture window. By second-cup coffee time, the window was filled with a dozen black and pink noses and eager eyes vying for window space to convey their enthusiasm for a warm spot in the kitchen.

"Oh, for God's sake, let them in," said Tessie.

"They thought you'd never ask," answered Art, getting up to open the door and call their eager guests in. Soon the kitchen was filled with wagging tails and bodies of all sizes and colors, nudging their hosts for a snack or scratch.

"Have any more butter?" asked Tessie. "Those muffins are delicious."

"Me too," echoed Sally, backhanding hers to a standard poodle with his nose under her apron.

"There's several pounds in the freezer in the woodshed. Just go through that door. It's right there. We keep the freezer out there so it doesn't burn electricity in winter."

From behind the door to the woodshed, Sally and Art both heard a loud shriek and a thud. Art raced out to see what had happened only to find Tessie lying in a heap on the floor in front of the freezer. The chest freezer lid was up and the light on.

Tessie stirred. "Oh, my God! What is that in there?" she cried as Art helped her to her feet.

Sally came rushing in and grasped immediately what had happened. You met "the tsarina." Her name is Anna. She died last fall of a strangulated intestine... happens a lot to the big sight hounds. She's a Russian wolfhound, a brindle Borzoi. Her owner's in India... long story. We put her in the freezer because her owner wants to give her a proper sky burial and say her good-byes when she comes back from Rajasthan in May. She believes in reincarnation — typical Stowe. When she gets home, we'll thaw her out and give her a good brushing. She'll look fine.

"My God, a dead dog in the freezer with food you eat?" Tessie gasped.

"She's wrapped in plastic. She can't hurt anything in there," Art offered.

"It's just... well, I ...."

"It's okay Mom. Now that it's winter, we thought about just hanging her up on the barn wall till spring, but as we learned from the chickens, a lot of critters winter in there as well so we decided the safest place was in the freezer. We get paid $15 a day regardless. That'll pay for the 300 maple syrup cans we'll need this spring when Art starts boiling."

Lost Key

"STILL WANNA GO riding?" she asks.

"Sure, I've got four days off before I have to go back to work in Island Pond for the last time."

"Come on up tomorrow afternoon. You know where our farm is in the Hollow?"

"I think so. Isn't it the white farmhouse with a big porch below Farnham's Hill with the apple trees on the right?"

"That's it."

"See you around two"

"Wear jeans."

The phone returns a dial tone. He hangs there for a few minutes as the phone buzzes. He sees Tina again leaning against the paddock fence next to him in her jeans with strands of hay still in her hair.

The next day, he heads off in his black VW bug. Through the widening rust holes in the sheet metal floor, he can see the dirt road change to asphalt as he veers onto Route 100 toward Stowe. The Hollow Road leads up into the backcountry at the base of the Worcester Range. A few persistent hill farmers, not yet fallen prey to urban skiers looking for quaint farms or ski clubs looking for cheap accommodation during the season, still eke out a living.

The road winds by the base of Farnham Hill. The disheveled white farmhouse he remembered as the Curlin Farm sits near a grove of ancient, unpruned apple trees spiked with water shoots and rich with small apples abandoned to the abundant population of deer. Local hunters use the orchard as an observation point to assess and track bucks for later in the season.

He parks in the yard next to an old Dodge Power Wagon stripped to its frame but with a newish hardwood bed and rusted winch assembly. A few other hulks are settled into the boggy lawn between the porch and Gold Brook, which runs by the house a few yards away. Tina steps out on the sloping porch as he climbs the steps and greets him with a beguiling smile.

"No trouble finding the place?" she asks.

"No, I remembered it from when we used to fish in Gold Brook and from going up to the Marsters' swimming hole when they were away."

"You don't have any riding boots, I guess," she says, looking ruefully at his worn penny loafers.

"These'll have to do," he apologizes. "I told you I don't ride much."

"Well, let's saddle up Becky for you, and Favreau for me."

"Favreau. That's a fancy name for a horse. He or she from France?" he asks, smiling.

"No. He's a gelding named after my Uncle Favreau on my mother's side. That was her maiden name."

"How is your dad?" he asks.

"He's okay when he's not drinking," she answers matter-of-factly.

Tina hands him a western saddle and indicates a chestnut mare with a toss of her head.

David heaves the saddle into place and cinches the sheepskin-lined girths. He then lowers his stirrups and turns to watch Tina do the same. She's wearing dark caramel riding boots, tight jeans and a partially unbuttoned white blouse. The décolletage frames her loosely confined breasts, which shift beneath her blouse as she tosses the saddle onto Favreau's broad back. Tina then leads both horses into the yard and tethers their bridles to the remains of a post-and-rail fence. Becky's mouth fills with white foam as she worries the chrome bit in her mouth. Favreau is motionless. Tina disappears into the house. David hears a baby crying inside. An older woman raises her voice and the crying stops. Tina emerges with a wineskin hanging from her shoulder, runs down the steps, skipping several, untethers both horses, tosses him his reins, and swings herself up onto her horse. David mounts his horse after a couple of trial thrusts with his right leg.

"You'll be fine. Becky's a sweetheart. Just follow me for now until we get up into the hills."

The riders pass through the orchard and begin to climb slowly, zigzagging up the hill behind the farmhouse as they follow a barely discernible path into an old, sparse stand of sugar maples high above the farm.

"Dad used to sugar here until the bank finally took back the evaporator. He could only make his payments when he was selling to the ski lodges. It was okay as long as he made double payments to cover the other seven months, but the second year, it warmed up so fast in March that the sap stopped running early and Dad only made about seventy gallons. He could only make payments for three months. Poor bastard gave all the money to the bank from his sugar sales, even when we needed it. Dad's not very good with money ... always full of ideas ... works hard but never knows which bills to pay when ... pays whoever yells loudest and lends money to anyone who asks him."

"How many brothers and sisters do you have?" David asks, hoping the question will detour the conversation away from the family's hardships.

"Three now," she answers, without looking around. "Mom and Dad, bein' raised Catholic, never took to, you know, birth control and God knows couldn't imagine abstinence ... The family just kept growing when I was young ... seemed like there was always one in the oven. One died of that sudden infant death thing right in her crib and another, Johnny, was given to my Aunt to raise over in upstate New York. She couldn't have kids and we couldn't take care of what we had. So now, it's just me, Andy, Jenny, and Emma. Andy'll be outta here as fast as she can ... already's got a serious beau chasin' her."

He smiles, remembering the earnest disquisition of Sister Lamoureux in catechism about purity of thought and abstinence. She seemed barely old enough to understand the latter subject herself and yet was the quintessence of the former in her black habit. She was an extraordinary beauty even though her radiant light skin was evident only within the confines of the stiff wimple that framed her face and pressed into her temples. The cognitive dissonance between her strict articulations on moral rectitude in catechism and the sensual beauty of her smile when she led them in prayer with her hands pressed together between her breasts left the girls enraptured, imagining their own saintly virginity and the garrulous boys torn between hope of salvation and their lascivious fantasies about her.

"Mom had the late life surprise when Emma was born last year," Tina continues. As they emerge from the stand of maples, many with rusty taps still in place, they come into a clearing with a small brook running through on their left. The brook has been dammed with fieldstones to create a backwater deep enough to allow animals to drink.

"Let's let the horses drink," Tina says, dismounting in one move and setting the wineskin on the moss.

He follows suit and both lead their horses over to the brook. "No need to tether 'em, they won't wander away," Tina says, sitting down on a mound of moss near the brook and spreading out her long legs.

"Sit down and tell me who you are," she says, taking a shot from the wineskin and handing it to him. "Have some. Nothing fancy."

"I often wonder," he answers, taking the wineskin.

"You grew up in Mo'ville didn't you?"

"Yeah, from the age of two."

"Your dad used to be an instructor at the mountain, I saw Alain on weekends ... handsome guy."

"That's right. Then he settled into his management job in Eden at the asbestos mine. What does your dad do?" he asks.

"Whatever he can. Right now he's a hired hand at the Gale Farm on the Mountain Road and keeps their equipment runnin'. Won't milk, though — draws the line at pullin' teat. We all worked as soon as we were old enough. Lotta mouths to feed," she answers. "He's started drinking again, though, and missin' work. I'm not lookin' forward to him losing his job 'cause Mom's sugar's gettin' worse."

"Sorry," David says, lying back and staring up into the crowns of the nearby maple trees. Tina rolls onto her side with her chin cupped in her hand to look at him.

"Bet some of these trees are over a hundred years old," he observes, "That one over there must be a hundred feet. Look at all the old taps still in it. Bitch hitting sugar taps with your chainsaw ... ruin the chain."

"My grandfather used to tap these trees," Tina observes.

"You on ski school or patrol?" he asks after a long silence.

"Both ... whatever they want," she answers. I'm never sure when I get there for the milk run what I'll be doing that day. My favorite time, though, is dusk. We all trail-sweep after the lift closes and the mountain is empty. Far below, I can see the stream of headlights leaving and winding down through the valley. The sun sets quickly in winter and I feel alone on the mountain. On the last run, I can hear the stillness and the tree limbs creaking as the temperature drops with the sun. By the time I reach the base lodge, it's often dark … best time of day."

She asks about David's summer job and he tells her about the black flies and how sometimes they run out of fly dope and just rub bar and chain oil on their arms. How at the end of the day, it would often be an hour or so before they could hear one another without shouting, after the din of the saws stopped ringing in their ears. He tells her about the tall hemlock that fell on Ray when the wind caught it and how, when they finally cleared the brush away and found him, he pretended to be dead, and how angry they all were when he opened his eyes and winked at them.

Through the branches he watches two red-tailed hawks gyre in the sky. One suddenly plummets to the open meadow and, just as suddenly, flies off, pumping its wings with a baby rabbit in its talons. Both hear the shriek of the prey.

She tells David how once they saw from the window in their kitchen in late winter a pack of wild dogs running down an exhausted doe whose sharp hooves penetrated the deep snow, making escape impossible, while the dogs ran on the surface with their spreading paws. And how, after a hard winter, the deer herd is weakened from lack of food and many fall prey to wild dogs.

As he tells her of his hope of one day owning a team of draft horses, she drops her elbow and rolls toward him, kissing him long on the lips. Her lips seek his neck and his chest, and then return to his mouth. He has never been kissed this way. Fear and pleasure rise in him and he doesn't know how to reciprocate.

"Just relax," she whispers. "I'll do all the work. Just enjoy yourself."

"I can't," he mutters.

"Yes, you can," she whispers.

"What if we get pregnant?" he says.

"I can promise you, you won't," she whispers back. "Take it easy, it's fun."

"I have to go," he says.

She rolls onto her back.

"You don't want me?"

"Of course, I do," he answers.

"I'm not pretty?"

"You're beautiful," he stammers.

"Then why are you leaving?"

"I promised I'd be back."

"Promised who?"

"My mother," he answers, embarrassed.

"Is she prettier than me?" she retorts archly.

"It's not that," he allows, embarrassed. "It's just that I've never ...."

"I know. It's all right. It's fun. I'll show you," she urges.

David gets to his feet. "You are the most beautiful person I've ever seen. I would love to, but I can't. I have to go."

And with that he walks down the hill toward the farm, leaving his horse with Tina. Lying back on the moss, she calls after him, "See you soon."

The horses nibble at the short grass near the brook. Tina hums a Hank Williams tune and watches squirrels chasing one another in the maple branches high above.

Half an hour passes and Tina is drowsing off in the warm sun when she hears David yelling to her from the meadow below.

"Have you seen my car key? I thought I left it in the car, but I must'a put it in my pocket and dropped it. I've been looking all along the path we took. I always leave it in the car."

"Yup," she answers.

"Where is it?" he answers, breathless from the long uphill hike. He squats down next to her. "Did you find it?"

"You're lookin' right at it," she says.

"I don't get it. I really do have to get home."

"I know. But you'll have to find your key first," she says with a beguiling smile.

"I don't understand."

"It's inside me," she smiles softly, "Yours for the taking."

*   *   *

As the sun set over the Worcester Range, David and Tina ride down through the glade toward the farm. At the house, Tina puts the horses in the barn while David waits nervously to say goodbye and wonders if he should ask to see her again. He feels weak in the knees.

"Come on inside and meet my youngest sister," she says when she returns from the barn, "I know your Mom is waiting for you, but she can wait another few minutes."

With a hard pull, Tina opens the warped screen door into an expansive kitchen dominated by a large wood cookstove and an oak dining table with a number of mismatched chairs. An infant sits in a highchair, eating mashed peas and rice with her hands. She is watched over by a girl slightly younger than Tina.

"Meet my younger and nicer sis, Andy. Andy, this is David, he's from Mo'ville. I've just been teaching him to ride. Jenny's still at school. That's Emma in the high chair, she's my newest sister."

Andy is about 17 and shares her sister's beauty, although her features are sharper and her hair considerably darker. A woman well into her fifties ambles in from the living room in men's pants and a man's denim work shirt. A radio drones in the background.

"Say hi to David, Mom. We been ridin' in the high meadow."

"I 'spect you have," she says matter-of-factly. Without looking up, she pours herself some coffee from the dappled enamel coffee pot on the stove. "Wan' some coffee?"

"No, thanks, Mrs. Curlin, I gotta get home and get ready for work up in Island Pond."

"What you do up there?" she asks.

"Work on a chainsaw crew."

"Dangerous work," she mutters, again without looking up. "You best take care."

"I will," he answers.

Emma bangs her cup on the wood tray that confines her in the high chair.

"Got to head out. Nice to meet you all. See you soon," he says to Tina. She follows him out to the car.

"Don't be a stranger. Call me."

"I will when I get back in two weeks," he answers.

"I like you," Tina says, sticking her head inside the VW window with a broad smile.

"Me, too," he answers.

Later that week, while limbing a downed white pine, it occurs to him that Mrs. Curlin is too old to be Emma's mother.

Bakin' for
the Bacon

DAVID REMEMBERS WHEN he was eleven and he was left in Eugénie's care for the afternoon while Alain took Helen, Paul, and Juliette to Burlington to buy new school clothes at the outlet store. Eugénie is baking bread. In a large, dark brown ceramic bowl, she kneads a dark dough. She adds a cup of raisins and over-ripe banana pieces and begins kneading again. David is used to seeing her gnarled hands work white dough, then set it out to rise by the stove, knead it once more before shaping it into loaves, pat the loaves into her black sheet-metal bread pans, and slide them into a hot oven.

David asks about the color of the loaves. Eugénie explains that this is the day her brother-in-law, Benoit, will come to kill and butcher her three pigs and that the loaves are for the pigs. Confused, David asks why she bakes bread for pigs that are going to die. "All in good time," she answers.

Less than an hour later, Eugénie removes the hot loaves from her gas oven and the room fills with the rich smell of hot molasses. The three loaves cool for a bit on a rack and then she removes them from their pans, setting them side-by-side so they just fill an enamel refrigerator bin. From below her kitchen sink she takes an unopened quart of Nova Scotia screech, a cheap dark rum named for the behavior it induces among those who drink it to excess. She pours the entire bottle onto the three loaves and leaves them to soak up the brown fluid.

Uncle Ben arrives with his truck after lunch and sets up an old cast-iron enamel bathtub on four cinder blocks in the backyard. Underneath he builds a roaring fire of dry pine branches, adding hardwood logs when the fire is going. With a hose from the tap on the side of the house, he fills the tub with water. He hangs a come-along from the garage doorway, lays a maple slab the size of a coffee table across two sawhorses, and arranges a selection of wood-handled knives.

After coffee and doughnuts inside, Eugénie and David bring the three loaves out to the pigpen behind the house. The three eager Berkshires are hungry and Eugénie hands each sow a dripping loaf of her freshly baked molasses bread. David watches in astonishment as each sow snuffles up her loaf in less than a minute and then, after looking at each other to make sure there are no leftovers to tussle over, lies down in the mud to savor and digest her treat. Several minutes later, the three pigs are drooling in the mud and snoring peacefully.

Uncle Ben is soon joined by his son Bruno who is carrying a Remington .30-06 deer rifle. With a nod from Eugénie, who looks away and crosses herself, Bruno lodges two bullets above the snout and between the closed eyes of each sleeping pig. The gunfire does not wake them.

When the pigs cease their twitching and their hind legs quit mimicking an escape, Uncle Ben and Bruno wrestle one of the 250-pound sows over to the water bubbling gently in the bathtub and flop her in, displacing considerable water. After a few minutes of scalding, the men drag the carcass to the come-along, slipping its large hook through the heel tendons and cranking the pig up high enough for to scrape the bristles and begin butchering. The first incision is across the neck and the dark blood spurts out into a stainless steel milking bucket. The blood will be saved to make Eugénie's signature *boudin noir*. Benoit makes another incision from the anus to the neck and scoops out and severs the internal organs, and drops them into another milking bucket for later sorting. Bruno saws the open carcass in half and lays the halves on the maple slab while his father begins with the largest knife to cut them into quarters.

The laborious process is repeated twice and it's dinnertime before the last quarter is wrapped and tied up in butcher paper and loaded onto the truck.

David's father and mother stop by on their way home to pick him up, sparing a few minutes for conversation with Eugénie, Benoit, and Bruno before heading home.

The Forcier Farm

THE FORCIER FARM covered a large section of the Elmore Mountain Road. The gentler incline falling away from the mountain to the dirt road named after it had been cleared of trees and brush into hayfields. At the upper edge of the sloping fields where the incline steepened significantly, the sugarbush began with its ancient stand of maples. Their interlocking crowns blocked out the sun, discouraging all undergrowth except a waist-deep sea of ferns. This made the movement of horse and sledge easy going among the maples when sap collection began in late February or early March, depending on the weather. From 480 taps the sweet water dripped into rusting buckets as the sap rose with the daytime temperature. The sugarworks was too steep for Etienne's tractor, but his team had little difficulty negotiating the steep moraine slopes. The mountain with its westerly exposure and sweeping views of Mansfield and Sterling also provided some high pasture areas, while the lower fields cleared by Alcide Forcier two generations earlier produced an abundance of hay for their herd of mixed Jerseys and Holsteins.

As with many hill farms, the steeper inclines presented a danger to farmers who had made the switch from team to tractor. To avoid erosion and runoff they had to furrow or spread manure laterally on all possible inclines. Some fields were simply too steep. On these Etienne had planted apple trees, knowing that if all else failed, he could rely on sugar and apples to get him through a bad dairying year, of which there had been several since the co-op price of milk did not offset the rising prices for feed grains, kerosene, and gas. The county Extension agent had been out on his rounds to explain to Etienne the new bulk milk cooling system requirements coming in the fall: he would have to retire his tinned milk cans and spend the price of a new tractor on the newly mandated milk storage system. The co-op advanced their members the money to acquire the stainless steel tank and refrigeration equipment and recovered the money over time from their weekly milk checks. Etienne neither liked nor understood the canned speech by the Extension agent, and like his neighbors, he ignored the mandate until it was upon him. Weather and government, the two variables in farming, were the topics of conversation among farmers on the few occasions when they encountered one another at church, the feed store, or the monthly Grange meetings.

There were three Forcier boys, two of whom were twins, and an older daughter named Clarisse. The youngest son, Marcel, was 8th grade and was branded by his teacher Mrs. Odie as "fractious. He was often the subject of disciplinary actions ranging from visits to the principal's office to classroom humiliations that entertained his peers.

Marcel seemed immune to these castigations, and even to the apocalyptic threats of Father Lefèvre and his flock of visiting nuns from Quebec who came on Saturdays to teach catechism. To the surprise of all, however, he treated elders with respect when addressing them. He did not sass or talk back. He simply did as he wanted regardless of the admonitions of elders. The only daunting figure in his life was his father, himself a retired hellion. Marcel behaved impeccably at home on the farm, where he worked hard to improve the family's lot.

One of the twins, Robert, had died in a farming accident several years earlier. A contretemps with his strict father had left the quiet 12-year-old alone outside finishing a chore before supper. The larger of their two Farmall tractors was backed up to one of the two banded-stave silos at the west end of the barn. The night before, his father had connected the tractor's PTO drive shaft to the augur-fed corn chopper and had left Robert to finish hand-feeding an adjacent wagonload of corn stalks into the augur that chopped the stalks into silage and fed it up into the silo.

A stiff wind came up after supper and the temperature dropped. Robert went into the house to get his woolen jacket. He returned and had resumed the repetitive chore of feeding the long stalks into the augur when it caught the loose flap of his unbuttoned coat.

Soon after, his mother came out to call him for supper and saw he was gone and the tractor was still running. Puzzled, she climbed onto the tractor, killed the ignition and then climbed down and called her husband.

Dusk had become twilight and her husband was finishing milking in the barn. He emerged with a lantern to see what the trouble was. His anger rose as he strode toward the tractor and he assembled the harsh English words he would have with his son who had left farm equipment running unattended. Only when he set the lantern down near the PTO shaft did he see the blood-soaked ground beneath the augur and the shreds of his son's clothing in the side bearings. He grasped his wife, who had not seen this and said to her in their native language, "A la maison! J'ai à te dire!!" Etienne only spoke French when he was at a loss for a way to frame a thought in his limited English. Annette burst out crying as he hustled her toward the unlit farmhouse and screamed, "What 'appened?" Just as no one had heard Robert's short cry for help over the running tractor, there were no neighbors close enough to hear Mrs. Forcier's choking sobs and shouted recriminations through the night.

The funeral service was attended by well over half the townsfolk. A family's loss of a child overwhelmed conventional religious and social boundaries. People spilled out onto the stairs and lawn around Holy Family Catholic Church during the brief service. Only the family's close friends accompanied them to the interment at St. Ann's hillside cemetery outside of Hyde Park. St Ann's was the final resting place for most of the local *habitants*.

Marcel, Clarisse, and Leo, the surviving twin, had been picking early apples on the hill above the westernmost fields. The Macs and Winesaps were plentiful that year, though only the Macs were ready for picking. The trio had filled 16 wooden crates. Marcel headed off to get the tractor and wagon to haul them back. His father had warned him about using the tricycle-wheeled tractor on the orchard's steeper inclines and forbidden him from driving the tractor into the sugarworks. Marcel was careful, driving the tractor up the hill to where his sister and brother had amassed the crates. He parked the idling tractor and the three of them loaded the full crates onto the wagon. Clarisse and Leo climbed onto the wagon and waved to Marcel. Leo, noticing that they had left a picking pole leaning in a tree, hopped off and went over to get it. Marcel engaged the second gear and began to turn the tractor around slowly to follow the same path back to the barn.

In the brief moment when the tractor was perpendicular to the incline, it tipped over. Clarisse felt what was coming and jumped off on the uphill side. Marcel, trying to stabilize the tipping tractor turned the wheel sharply. Then he tried to jump off the uphill side as well, but his loose rubber barn boot caught under the clutch. The tractor rolled twice down the hill bringing the attached wagon and apple crates with it and Marcel was pinned under the right rear wheel.

Leo stayed with Marcel, who was conscious, while Clarisse ran to get her father who was in the milk shed cleaning milk cans. Etienne told her to run into the house and tell her mother to get help quickly while he gathered a wooden half plank, a car jack, a log chain and one of the horses grazing behind the barn.

When they reached the orchard, Marcel had passed out but was still breathing, though erratically. Leo was talking to him but to no avail. The tractor had stalled and gasoline dripped from its air filter housing. The four-foot wheel with its attached cast-iron wheel weights for stability lay on Marcel's pelvis and lower rib cage. An earlier effort by Leo to extract his brother had elicited such cries of pain that he had stopped.

Paying no attention to his son, Etienne laid the plank down next to him and placed the jack on it. He settled the lip of the bottle jack against the tire rim and furiously began moving the lever up and down. The plank pressed into the earth as it began to assume the weight of the tractor and slowly the fender and wheel began to lift enough so that Etienne and Leo could slide Marcel out. His legs did not lie as they should and Etienne realized that he could not get his son on the horse. He sent Leo running to the shed for the canvas tarpaulin he used to cover the side rake or tedder when he left them in the field at night. The three of them then managed to carry Marcel, who was groaning and still unconscious, back to the farmhouse where they laid him on the floor of the kitchen. His mother covered him with a quilt and spoke softly to him in her native French.

Shortly thereafter a neighbor arrived in his Dodge pickup with a metal bedstead in the back. They brought the bed into the kitchen, got Marcel on it and then replaced it in the bed of the truck. Etienne and his wife climbed into the back of the truck and their nearest neighbor, Chris Jensvold, drove off to Copley Hospital where Doc Chapin had been alerted and would be waiting at the door with two nurses.

The truck bumped along on the dirt road and Marcel's frequent moans through his unconsciousness left his mother sobbing as she sought to comfort him. Etienne just stared at the boy and wondered if he was to lose another son to the farm he had worked so hard to provide for his family and had loved in spite of the toll it exacted.

Marcel reappeared in class seven weeks later in a wooden wheelchair. It was after the first snows had blanketed the farm and the winter-long fire had been lit in the Sam Daniels furnace in the cellar beneath their farmhouse. He greeted his classmates with a familiar but subdued bravado and seemed anxious to tell the tale of how he had ended up in a "rolling chair." He told his story many times, always ending with the punch line, "How ya like dem apples?"

Four weeks later he was negotiating crutches, but his crushed pelvis and left hip joint would never heal well enough to allow him to walk without them, dashing his hopes of someday taking over his father's farm. Leo was the only male left and, in time, would have to choose whether his childhood dream of a military career would fall to the unspoken obligation to manage the farm. The Viet Nam War draft made his decision for him and, after basic training, Leo was in the jungles of Viet Nam fighting VCs, snakes, insects, fungal infections and, finally, an addiction to heroin, to which he waved a white flag. Only part of him came home.

Women did not inherit working farms in those days and, in any case, Clarisse had made known to her parents her intent to take Holy Orders and enter the cloistered convent in Richmond. Her brother's return home from 'Nam left her no choice but to sell or maintain the farm herself. Farms were first off the place where families lived and grew up together and, if they were lucky and industrious, a sustaining business as well. To realize a home and a living from 40-odd acres of land was increasingly rare.

The burden of stewardship on young Clarisse was amplified by her father's insistence on burying what remained of Robert in the orchard and her knowledge that the ground near the silo was macerated in his blood.

Since his accident, Marcel had had a succession of menial jobs, all of which he lost when he took to drink. Later that year with no place to stay, he moved back home under Clarisse's stipulation that he give up alcohol altogether. The state paid for the wooden ramp that he needed to get his wheel chair up and down the front porch.

Meanwhile, Leo was in and out of the VA Hospital in White River, and Clarisse made clear that she would let him come home if the Army could wean him from the drug habit he acquired while in his country's service. Like so many, Clarisse had seen little point to the war, in fact, to any war since the one her father had fought in Europe before she was born.

Farming came naturally to the young redhead for whom marital subservience to another farmer or, if she chose, to Christ, had seemed the only options. Clarisse ran the farm, ignoring traditions and improving the processes on which her father and most of his family had survived. Her neighbor and extension agent, Silas Jewett, himself a farmer, was always on hand to explain some new farming method or practice and to help when a daunting problem developed. In time, she earned the respect of her skeptical male peers, adding to her land, and acquiring equipment and additional dairy stock as needed. In greater Morristown the only other exception to farming men was a trio of sisters and their mother in Mud City. The Lepine women managed a thriving farm in the shadow of Sterling Mountain and, like Clarisse, felt no compunction to abandon their family homestead.

Leo returned home chastened after six months without drugs or drug surrogate, but still haunted by dreams of his time at war. Clarisse made clear that she ran the farm, but that Leo could, through hard work, earn back her trust and his equity in the enterprise.

Marcel applied himself to maintaining all the machinery on the farm. Leo built him a shop in the woodshed off the barn where he kept the complicated baling equipment running smoothly and maintained the two tractors, side rakes, plows, harrows, and all the complicated milking equipment. To augment their income, he took on random repairs for neighboring farmers when their own equipment went down.

Whether because of her beauty, her force of character, or her extensive property, Clarisse had several offers of marriage over the years. None of the men putting themselves forward tempted her as partners and she remained content to manage the Forcier Farm with her two surviving brothers. When Parkinson's disease began to take its toll on her mobility, she realized her childhood dream to wed her first intended and joined the convent in Richmond, leaving management of the farm to Leo, who had just married, and to Marcel. Together, the men managed the farm for several years more until the following generation of Leo's children took over.

Jeeter Gets His Buck

JEETER WAS ON the Overseer of the Poor's list of folks to whom Duke, the County Game Warden, would occasionally bring fresh roadkill.

When tourists or flatlanders hit a deer on the road, they'd wait for the police to come by or flag down a local and ask them to call a trooper to file an accident report so they could collect collision insurance and repair their damaged car. The deer, dead or alive, got little attention until the game warden showed up, fired a coup de grace, gutted and cleaned it, cutting away any damaged meat, and delivered the carcass to someone in need or to the County Poor Farm

Vermonters' priorities often differed, however, from those of their visitors. Forty to sixty pounds of good meat was a godsend. If the deer was injured enough not to leave the scene of the accident, the indigenous driver, risking prosecution, would dispatch the deer promptly, field dress it, toss the offal into the woods, the carcass in the trunk, and, assuming the car or truck damage required only bodywork, drive home to hang the deer in a cool, out-of-the-way place. When the meat was secure, they'd use a dent puller or go to the local junkyard for a used fender to repair the damage. Few Vermonters could afford collision insurance, and in any case, the deductible was usually higher than the value of their vehicle.

In later years, when the county office of Overseer was replaced with a State welfare system, edible road kill usually found its way to local game dinners where roadkill was fed to tourists eager to brag to friends back home how they ate beaver, squirrel, bear, raccoon, crow or venison just like the natives.

Jeeter wasn't particularly fond of ice fishing or deer hunting, but each year, the camaraderie, stories, and hooch-filled evenings invariably drew him to someone's shanty or deer camp. During deer season, his only weapon was the .410 shotgun his father left him, which he kept loaded with a single slug. He'd taped an old scope to the barrel but had never figured out how to sight the scope to a target so the scope amounted to little more than a hood ornament and an object of amusement to the hunters with whom he drank at night.

As the party headed out an hour before sunrise, Jeeter would rouse himself and tag along. When the hunters went their separate ways to favorite spots or to a clearing where they'd last seen a buck, Jeeter would fortify himself with some "dog hair," as he called his morning quaff, and settle down on a fallen tree trunk to wait for a buck to amble by. His comrades who were not tracking a buck would reconvene around lunch time at deer camp for some sandwiches, a nap, and then a final few hours of hunting before sunset.

If Jeeter was not awakened by a passing buck, he'd discharge his weapon for effect and return to camp for some soup and a sandwich of day-old Bunny Bread slathered with some of Egnor's pork fat and sprinkled liberally with sugar he'd poured into his jacket pocket while having a coffee at Paine's Restaurant. This was his favorite sandwich. He'd show off the empty breach to his smiling pals and tell how he muffed his best shot, blaming it on the scope.

That fall, Duke brought Jeeter a roadkill doe. Jeeter rushed over to his friend Egnor's cellar hole across the road and banged on the bulkhead door.

"Got us a new one," Jeeter announced, "... hangin' in my woodshed now. C'mover and see 'er... nice sammich doe, small 'un... little, but'll make great Bambiburgers. Duke just brung 'er over and 'splained where'n he got 'er from up to Stowe."

Egnor climbed out and stretched with a loud yawn. The chest hairs growing through his tee shirt indicated his bachelor status. He followed Jeeter over to his woodshed and examined the yearling.

"By the way," asked Jeeter, "Where's your guard goose, Milton?"

"I'se throwin' ma hearin' aid batteries away in the yard and he et 'em all. Think 'ey killed 'im."

"I'll shoot a shoat in a week or two when yer doe's had a chance to cure some and we can start grinding meat for the winter. Good timin'."

"Deer season starts in a few weeks, and I may get me a buck, too."

"Sure, like when I finish my first floor! You don't even have tags.

Nobody can see through that scope and, if you could, you'd probably shoot a deer follerin' ya. The day you shoot a buck'll be the day *Our Miss Brooks* moves into my finished two-story house."

Jeeter heard Egnor's bulkhead door fall shut with a metallic crash and hurt by his friend's disdain for his deer hunting skills, took a long sip of screech,.

Three weeks later to the day was the first day of deer season. Jeeter always earned extra grocery money for winter stores in the late fall, tipping for Tommy Lathrop over in Johnson. Tommy was a logger during most of the year but made most of his money with his thriving Christmas tree, wreath and garland business. He'd load up both log trucks with trees and wreaths and head for his spot on 78th and West End Avenue in Manhattan where he'd fleece city folk for his seasonal greens until the last tree was gone. He drove one truck and his wife Annie drove the other. They'd sell 24 hours a day for three weeks, taking turns sleeping in a truck's cab, often returning home with several thousand dollars in cash.

Jeeter would cash in each season for a modest share of Tommy's take by gathering fir tips for him and Annie from the neglected and overgrown Christmas trees he'd planted several years back hoping to sell to folks in Stowe. His dream was dashed when he went out to survey the trimming he'd done the previous day under the influence of screech.

His 200 balsams looked nothing like the nice conical shapes he'd seen in the tree catalog. He tried with his pruners to bring some of the damaged firs back to shape, but soon gave up. As the trees shot up, they began to look somewhat better, but as Egnor explained, few holiday revelers would be looking for 12-15-foot Christmas trees.

In a desperate attempt to save his investment in the 200-heel-ins he'd planted, he cut down three dozen firs and cut off the top third, leaving the bottoms where they fell. The trees looked passable but when he got to town his spot had been taken and he sold the trees to a fellow from Eden for half price, spent the proceeds at the State Store and drove home. His Christmas tree farm is now a thriving winter deeryard and he makes a $150 or so each year selling several dozen bales of tips to Tommy for his wreaths.

When anyone needed to get in touch with Jeeter, they called and left a message with Luther, the postman. One the first day of deer season, Luther stopped by Jeeter's to tell him his brother had called, hoping he'd come over and help him get his firewood in. Jeeter rarely heard from his brother except when he needed help, but always responded, as his brother had lost a leg in the War and lived alone on veteran's benefits. The two spent the day getting three cords of dry wood into the shed off the kitchen and then shared a couple of pints of blackberry-flavored brandy Luther kept handy for his brother's visits.

Jeeter left around 7:30 and wound his way along Route 12 through the Worcester Woods towards Elmore. On the Symonds Hill Road between Elmore and Wolcott, a spikehorn jumped out into the wash of his one headlight and froze. Neither Jeeter's brakes nor his brandy-macerated nerves were up to the task of a sudden stop and Jeeter heard the right fender crumple as it hit the buck.

He jumped out of the pickup and stared at the twitching deer. He opened his pocket knife, slit the buck's throat, and watched as the quivering deer bled out on the dirt road. Jeeter had never field dressed a deer before so he wrestled the 110-pound animal into the back of his truck and raced home as a plan took shape in his head.

When he got home he was exhausted. He got into bed in his long underwear and slept for a few hours. The excitement of his plan, however, animated his dreams and had him up, if groggy, well before dawn. He took a pull of "dog hair" and went outside.

Dragging the deer over to a nearby maple, he threw a rope over the lowest branch. He fed the rope through two small incisions he made behind the rear hooves and then pulled the deer up until its nose left the ground. He then made a clean cut from the anus down to the gullet. He cut and pawed out all the organs and fibrous tissue, leaving them in a pile on the ground nearby.

The sun was now rising in the sky. Jeeter lowered the deer back to the ground and dragged it over to the woodpile where he leaned it up lopsided against the stacked wood. He ran inside and fetched his .410, grateful that he'd remembered he'd need a kill shot to show off.

His aim didn't allow for much distance so, standing fifteen feet from the badly listing deer, he pulled the trigger and fired a shot into the spikehorn's right shoulder. He was surprised to see the damage done by the single slug. He pulled out the shell and realized he'd fired a high-power turkey load instead of the slug.

Egnor heard the discharge and came over just in time to see the gutted deer slump to the ground next to the woodpile.

"I got one. I got one. First day a deer season... I got me a buck."

Egnor looked at the empty deer carcass lying on the ground and then at Jeeter's truck, while his beagle, Rufus, sniffed at the still steaming pile of organs nearby.

"You drop 'im with that '52 Dodge. That half-ton rust bucket still packs a punch... bastard, one hell of a weapon. Sure as shit, that blunderbuss of yours didn't break that buck's right leg and shoulder. You got tags for your kill?"

"I ain't gonna report 'im. You 'n me'll butcher 'im. What I need tags for?"

"Thought you'd probly wanna show 'im 'round ta yer huntin buddies."

"Y'ain' gonna tell no one, is ya?" Jeeter asked suspiciously.

"If you and I'se gonna b'eatin' 'im, we'd best put 'im inside with th'other. I'll just have ta shoot two pigs now to make that venison edible. Them sammich deers is too lean by 'emselves. We'll have to borrow some space in Norma's chest freezer, too. We'll have 'nough meat for the next two years, even givin' her some for usin' her freezer. She likes Bambiburgers. C'mon, let's get it in the shed with th'other un."

When deer season ended, Egnor and Jeeter set up their rig for meat processing. Jeeter had his mother's hand-crank grinder clamped to a large sheet of plywood.

Egnor had shot, scalded, dressed, and cut into small pieces his two young pigs, all but the prime cuts, which he'd sell to Patch's market. The two cubed up the venison and with four animals in all, they had a small mountain of meat to grind by hand.

Egnor fetched a bucket of apple pomace from the cider mill. At the end of deer season they gave it away to anyone who wanted it, as many hunters would use it illegally to attract deer. But Egnor and Jeeter ground it in with the pork and venison. As the tub gradually filled with the blend of venison, pork and apple, Jeeter poured in a bottle of Karo Syrup and started to mix the mash with a baseball bat.

When the mash was complete and thoroughly mixed, the two rolled out piles of chopped meat into log-shaped rolls the same length as the freezer's width. They then placed each log carefully into the freezer and separated the layers with cardboard cut from old grocery boxes. The "meat logs" were about the diameter of a truck piston and would freeze up solid overnight.

"Christ, we'll have a half-cord 'a meat when we'se done this," noted Egnor. Jeeter nodded enthusiastically. When the woodshed freezer was full to the top, they packed the rest of the formed meat logs into boxes and drove it over to Norma's to add to the freezer on her front porch, telling her she could eat all she wanted in payment.

There was no shortage of meat that winter. The convenience of removing a meat log from the freezer and sawing off the requisite number of patties with a bucksaw and tossing the uncut piece back in while Bambiburger patties sizzled in a cast iron skillet on the woodstove made a hard winter easier.

Sphincter

GROW AND ALYSSA moved to Wolcott during the hippie migration of the late sixties. Enamored of the writings of Helen and Scott Nearing, they imagined building a house out of local stone and living off food foraged from the wild, as described in Euell Gibbons classic, *Stalking the Wild Asparagus*. Their bible was *The Whole Earth Catalog*. In Brooklyn, they heard that in Vermont one could find a small corner of the wild and simply move in, not having to bother with the capitalist nonsense of ownership, titles, and boundaries.

On their arrival, they found a gentle clearing on which to settle just off East Elmore Road. The dirt two-track meanders between the more cosmopolitan town of Wolcott and a nonexistent town called East Elmore. The small rise they chose turned out to be a bit spongy in wet weather, but there were no neighbors and the teepee kit they'd ordered from *The Whole Earth Catalog* went up in less than half a day.

Crow, né Norman Kravitz, and Alyssa, née Mona Selvig, loved their new home. Crow would find a job in Wolcott or Hardwick and Mona would tend the garden and forage for edibles in the nearby woods where they had already found an abundance of wild apples, grapes, and mushrooms. When they had an excess of either, they would drive "Kerouac," their VW microbus, into town and trade with locals for flour, sugar, and coffee.

During his job search in Wolcott, Crow had foraged an outdated *News and Citizen* and read a feature about the Vermont Arts Council. He was quite certain after reading the article that his plan to travel the countryside in Kerouac, staging dramatic tableaux to inspire and teach Vermont farmers how to live off the land would elicit a generous grant. The tableaux would feature Helen and Scott Nearing, Euell Gibbons, and Wendell Berry and his theater experience at The Guerilla Theater Company of Soho would inspire the production. Although this application was rejected, Crow was not discouraged and began work on another application that would help natives appreciate the unique flavors and health benefits of a vegetarian diet. To his surprise, this grant, too, was rejected, but Crow was undaunted. He soon found a job in Bettis's junkyard in Wolcott for $1.85 an hour, rewinding burned-out generators.

After several weeks of living on foraged food, Alyssa came down with what their only neighbor, Luther, called "the green-apple-quickstep." Crow had spent his last two weekends digging and constructing a privy to accommodate his wife's distressed bowels, and, although the directions in *The Whole Earth Catalog* were quite clear, the materials list called for items that Crow could not find in the wild, so he harvested a few boards and hand-cut nails from a collapsed barn nearby.

The following day while in Ron Terrill's Texaco in Morrisville chatting up Chet about the legalization of marijuana, Crow slipped into the men's room when Chet left to gas up a customer, unscrewed the toilet seat, and walked out with the seat under his arm. Chet saw the theft and assumed Crow must be a pothead; otherwise, why would anyone steal a badly stained and chipped toilet seat that needed replacing? He reported the odd event to Ron, but didn't bother to mention it to Officer Sargeant.

One morning in early fall, Crow and Alyssa awoke to the sound of a diesel tractor plowing furrows in the field just beyond their clearing. They dressed and wandered over to greet their neighbor in the way that they had learned rural neighbors greeted one another, by waving.

The driver of the tractor backed off the throttle on the roaring machine, shifted into neutral and then killed the engine as he watched the couple approach.

"Hello, there," Crow offered.

"Hello," came the response. "You two camping or what? Folks usually ask permission, but it's not tillable land yet, so it didn't bother me none if you camp there. How long you staying?"

"Oh, we live here now," Alyssa chirped.

"You do, do ya?" answered the driver. Who do you think owns the land, you're living on?"

"We assumed it was just wild land, maybe the people's land or state land or something... There's no one living around here much."

"All land is owned and you're squatting on my land... been in my family for three generations. My grandfather bought it with money it took him

32 years to save up. Come spring, I'll be out here with a bulldozer and brush hog clearing all these trees and making an open field of the woods around that teepee you're living in."

"We just moved here. What about our rights? That hardly seems neighborly."

"You're not neighbors. Neighbors are people who own land adjacent to one another. Pardon my language, but you don't own shit. You're on my land. How long you staying, again?"

Crow and Alyssa just stared at one another, surprised at the farmer's hostility.

"Tell you what... if you're still in that teepee in the spring, I'll give you the acre of land your living on, but you'll have to get used to tractor noise, 'cause come spring, you'll be surrounded by a hayfield. You city folks like views... well, you'll have a helluva view when all these trees is cut down and turned into lumber and firewood. See that black walnut over there. That bastard'll get me a fortune at the mill. Sleep tight now. My name's Cleveland, Dexter Cleveland. I live down the road a mile in case you and the missus need anything or get in trouble. Enjoy the fall while it lasts."

The tractor started with a roar and Dexter resumed plowing.

"Not a very nice man," pouted Alyssa as she returned to the teepee to boil water for her ginger tea. "Hardly my idea of neighborliness and loving the mother earth... bet he's never even read Rumi!"

As the nights got colder, Alyssa suggested to Crow that they get an electric heater. Crow reminded her that heaters needed an electrical outlet and began snoring.

Finally, in late November, the smoldering cooking fire the couple used to boil porridge and vegetables began to grow in size and smoke output. The inside of the teepee was black with smoke ash, as the smoke flap in the peak where the poles were bound together didn't open. Crow started sleeping outside in his down bag and Alyssa had taken to coughing. She soon joined him in his solo mummy bag, within which neither could move.

In early November, Luther dropped off a letter addressed to Mona Selvig, Rural Route Delivery, Wolcott, Vermont. Herald Butts, the postmaster, on a hunch, sent it to Luther to drop off to the only outsiders he knew of in his postal district. The letter was an invitation from Mona's mother to return to West Babylon, Long Island for Thanksgiving. Alyssa knew it for what it was. Her mother had not approved of her changing her name and heading off with the town's only hippie for parts unknown. Still, given the cold and her persistent intestinal distress, the invitation was enticing. Alyssa chose not to discuss the invite with Crow, who would, she knew, see it as a defeat.

While rummaging through Luther's trash, Crow came upon a recent *Future Farmers of America* magazine and some old UVM Extension brochures, one of which extolled the benefits of artificial insemination for engineering a more productive dairy herd.

Sensing a lucrative career opportunity, Crow pored over the brochure and sent away for more information about the company seeking representatives to offer this new service.

Sharing a sleeping bag designed for one had reduced his and Alyssa's sexual activity to an occasional outdoor rut on a sun-warmed mound of moss near the teepee, which they no longer used except to cook in or when it rained.

Crow tried to imagine cows having sex, his only knowledge of which was derived from personal experience, which was, to date, limited to the missionary position. The image he summoned was of a heifer lying on her back in the pasture with her legs in the air.

The following week, he met the Lamoille Country Extension Agent to learn more about the opportunity and to see firsthand how it worked. Crow was invited to meet the agent at the Metzger farm in Elmore where he had an appointment. As the agent prepared the tube of frozen bull semen for insertion and rolled up his sleeve, Crow asked, "top or bottom?"

The agent look confused. It finally dawned on him the import of Crow's question.

"The top hole is the sphincter, not much good putting it in there, it'll come right back at cha! It's the next hole down," he said, as he plunged his arm in full-length and deposited the tube. The blood drained from Crow's face as he turned away and the agent wiped down his arm with a wet hand towel.

Crow was unfamiliar with the term "sphincter" and betrayed his confusion. The agent explained it more casually, using the more common term, "asshole," although at this point it sounded more like an accusation than an explanation. The agent decided Crow was a hippie-pothead, said a curt goodbye, and left to chat with Joe Metzger whose heifer he had just inseminated.

Crow, now more confused than ever about the two options beneath the cow's tail and still trying again to imagine cows coupling missionary style, remembered suddenly that cows walk on all fours, whereas humans walk upright, and so began a slow arc of understanding about bovine anatomy. Crow climbed back into Kerouac, rolled another joint to clear his head of what he had just seen and made for home.

Just before the dream of living in nature died under an 18-inch snowfall right before Thanksgiving, Alyssa made friends with a "cute raccoon" that wandered into their teepee in search of food and friendship. She didn't notice the slathering drool hanging from its slack jaw, the advanced case of alopecia that had ravaged its pelt, or its uncharacteristic insouciance as it wandered into her presence.

Luther happened by to drop off another letter from her mother pleading for a response or at least a mailing address. He saw the animal, ran back to his pickup to grab the rifle mounted on his rear window, and dispatched the raccoon on the floor of the teepee with two shots from his 30.06.

Alyssa screamed as the animal dropped and began an involuntary running motion in its death throes.

"Y'er lucky, I'se here. That ain't no sweet little raccoon like you'se thinkin'. He's as rabid as our minister. I jes' saved ya from a dozen very painful shots in the gut. He's half-dead from rabies."

"What's rabies?" asked Alyssa, looking away from the now quiet animal.

"It's a disease wild animals and pets what's bit by 'em gets. Kills 'em 'ventually but their bite is deadly to people, too. S'why ya have to get the shots and you don' want 'em, trust me. I had to put down my beagle, Ralph, after he got bit by a rabid skunk. Got a shovel?"

Alyssa got a shovel from the outhouse where Crow kept his few tools, and Luther picked up the raccoon and carried it out of the clearing where, in the distance, Alyssa could hear him digging a hole in which to bury it, as she read her mother's newest plea to come home to West Babylon.

*   *   *

After the early snowfall brought down their shelter, Crow and Alyssa abandoned the collapsed teepee and growing pile of rocks they had gathered to begin their new home and rented a second-story apartment in nearby Morrisville. Crow landed a job in the Pease Grain Store, hauling 100-pound sacks of grain from warehouse pallets to a delivery truck. On weekends, he continued to re-wind generators that Bettis's wife, Betty, dropped off for him at the grain store. Pretty soon, Crow was making enough to afford his rent, the engine overhaul Kerouac needed, and store-bought food that helped Alyssa gradually regain mastery of her intestines.

With these new creature comforts and an innate sense of security came pregnancy. Heather was born the following summer, followed by Mead sixteen months later. As the family grew into their new community and the pages of their *Whole Earth Catalog* yellowed with age and their rural utopian paperbacks gathered dust on a shelf next to *The Joy of Cooking* and *Dr. Spock's Baby and Child Care*, Alyssa felt strongly that Heather and Mead should grow up with a pet of their own.

Remembering with pain the episode with the raccoon, Alyssa insisted they get a new-born kitten from someone in the community. Crow, still rapt by the idea of raising a wild orphan, was finally convinced and, several years later, when Heather was five and Mead four, Crow answered an ad for a free kitten and the family went together to pick out a male tiger kitten with double paws from a home on Maple Street.

They brought the two month-old kitten home in a shoebox, lined with one of Heather's old diapers. When they got home, Crow reached in and picked up the kitten by the scruff of the neck as its owner had shown him, and placed him on the linoleum kitchen floor, where he squatted down and promptly extruded a small turd.

"What'll we name him?" Mead asked.

Annoyed by the recent deposit on the kitchen floor, he hissed, "Should call the little fellow "Sphincter" after that performance!"

"What's a sphincter?" Heather chirped.

Having read in Spock that children always sense a evasion and that every question deserves a candid answer, and, drawing on his earlier confrontation with the extension agent, Crow explained in rather more detail than Alyssa would have preferred what a sphincter was and the role it played in the body.

Like most children his age, Mead, who had coined the term "fanny burp" when dissuaded from discussing farts, was delighted with the subject, and began chanting, "Phinxter, Phinxter."

He was soon joined by Heather and, after a whispered discussion by Alyssa and Crow in which they agreed that that the choice seemed innocuous enough, it was decided that the new kitten's name would be "Phinxter," the closest either child could come to pronouncing the word their father had explained, yet remote enough not to raise eyebrows among friends who also had children.

With parenthood came responsibility and the need to teach responsibility so Crow explained that Phinxter's caregivers would have to take him to the vet to get his shots and to be checked for worms. Heather nodded earnestly and Mead paid attention.

The following week, they drove to Dr. Walker's for his Saturday morning office hours. Heather cradled Phinxter in her lap and, when Dr. Walker beckoned them into the examining room, she carried him in and set him up on the padded table.

"What's your kitty's name?" the vet asked in an avuncular tone.

"Sphincter," Mead answered to the astonishment of his father. "I like your hat."

Crow was nonplussed, as was Dr. Walker, who looked up at Mead's father and queried, "Sphincter?"

Crow just nodded, adding," It's not a hat, sweetie. It's a toupee."

"What's a toupee?" Heather chirped.

"I'll tell you later," Crow said dismissively.

"Sphincter?" repeated Dr. Walker to Crow.

"Yes, that was the kitten's name...when..."

"Fine by me, just unusual," answered Dr. Walker as he wrote the name down on the form attached to his clipboard.

On the way home, Crow, still somewhat thrown by the encounter, decided to let the matter lie for the time being, but did explain to Heather about toupees and why one should never ask about them.

A year later, Alyssa was sorting through mail she had retrieved from their post office box and came across a small postcard that read:

"Dear Mr. Kravitz, It's time to bring your Sphincter in for a rabies shot. Please call for an appointment. Dr. Walker, Veterinarian.

Personal Injury Settlement

HARLEY BENSON, FLANKED by his two elected side judges, Ronnie Terrill and Lurleen Dumas, had seen all the courtroom antics a judge might see from his bench high inside the Hyde Park courtroom. There were few surprises after his years on the bench, administering local justice. Harley had, however, developed a particular antipathy toward absurdly high monetary jury awards and ambulance-chasers, of which Lamoille County had only one so far.

Jack Tyler first tasted the rich broth of a personal injury settlement when he took Mildred Hornby's case on contingency, since she couldn't raise the retainer he required of clients seeking financial redress in the courts. Nor did she have the wherewithal to pay his $35 an hour fee, so she gratefully acceded to his request for a 35% contingency on any potential jury award, which he was confident they would win given the circumstances of her complaint. Contingency fees had, by now, become standard in the more urbane courtrooms of Chittenden and Rutland Counties, much larger seats of justice.

Jack convinced Mildred she should sue Raymond Excavating when one of their dump truck drivers with what today are called "anger management issues," dumped twelve yards of wet gravel on Mildred's Dodge Dart after she touched her horn and the horn relay froze.

According to testimony gathered by Officer Billy Sargeant of the Morrisville Police Department—Billy was, in fact, the Morrisville Police Department—the truck driver was trying to open a beer bottle with a house key while stopped at a stop sign. After several minutes and no traffic to stop for, Mildred tapped her horn, the horn relay stuck, and the dump truck driver, unable to open the bottle, flew into a rage at the persistent horn, dumped his load on her, and drove off to refill it at the company's gravel pit and to fetch his church key from the glove compartment of his pickup.

Mildred was discovered about thirty minutes later by Volney Farr passing by on his tractor. He stopped, turned off his tractor, and heard her yelling inside the car. He gathered some local boys to help shovel her out.

When Jack Tyler saw the story in the *News and Citizen*, he sniffed a monetary award and paid Mildred a visit. Mildred did not thoroughly understand how the law worked in such cases and had assumed that the driver would be criminally charged and sentenced appropriately. She was, however, worried that her insurance policy might not cover the extensive damage to the finish of her car and its broken windshield.

When Jack completed his summation to the jury, Harley whispered to his side judges, "He should try out for the Lamoille County Players. He's got a talent for theater."

Jack's performance did convince an empathetic jury of the driver's "malice aforethought," the terrible trauma to "a respected widow-lady" and the need to "shower her with money to assuage the trauma of being buried alive and the damage to her personal property, of which she had little."

Mildred got $66,000 and Jack got $33,000 for the 36 "billable hours" he spent on the case.

"I ain't no fool," he regaled his astonished secretary. "Offer me $35 an hour or $900 an hour for the same amount of work... what's the question again?"

With a strong taste for contingency settlements in personal injury cases, Jack fitted himself out with a new pair of Hi-Tops for the ambulance chases yet to come. He also subscribed to and read all the area's local newspapers.

There were the usual run of accidents and mishaps, but when Jack "followed the money," the pot was often empty, until, in January, he read in *The Hardwick Gazette* that one Jeeter Parenteau had been admitted to the hospital with a dislocated shoulder and compound fracture in his arm because a truck tire he had been inflating blew apart. The accident landed Jeeter in the hospital for three days while doctors set, reset, and finally pinned his damaged humerus and radial bones.

Jack arrived in Jeeter's room during visiting hours the following evening with a wilting bouquet of mixed flowers bought at the Grand Union for 49 cents. Sensing that Jeeter was not a posy kind of guy he dropped the bouquet into Jeeter's water glass and expressed his most sincere condolences. Jeeter, who was staring ruefully at a scratched Melamine plate of food said without looking up, "I can't eat this shit." Trying to be tactful, Jack asked what was wrong with it. "Tough as boiled owl," Jeeter muttered looking up.

Jack soon sensed that Jeeter didn't need condoling as much as money, and his enthusiasm for the case accelerated as Jeeter told the story of how the tire "nearly blowed his arm off. Lucky to be 'live," he continued, thrilled to have an interested stranger to tell his story to.

A deal was struck in Jeeter's hospital room to file a civil lawsuit against Firestone Tire & Rubber, at that time number 25 on the Fortune 100 list of American companies ranked by assets. Jack began perusing brochures of Florida vacation villas and Jeeter began to dream of throwing away his siphon hose and buying gas at the pump whenever he needed it and placing an order with Peavine for a case of screech.

Jack filed the case in Hyde Park Superior Court for the plaintiff, one Jeeter Parenteau, seeking $500,000 in damages against Firestone Tire and Rubber in Akron, Ohio.

Personal injury suits were not new to Firestone and their legal department had a bevy of lawyers flying around the country defending product liability suits. Thomas Levy arrived in Burlington rented a car, bought a map and drove to Hyde Park, Vermont, which to his surprise had no motel or hotel. He found a room in nearby Morrisville at the recently built Sunset Motel where he kicked off his shoes, hung up his shirts, and began to review the plaintiff's deposition.

The court docket in Hyde Park was sparse and the case went to trial the following Monday after jury selection. Much to the dismay of Mr. Levy, the sparse crop called for jury duty were mostly women, as farmers were routinely excused from jury duty, especially during the summer months. To his further dismay, most of the women were elderly and he knew from courtroom experience that older women were usually sympathetic to plaintiffs, regardless of the underlying merits of the claim.

After the ten-woman, two-man jury was sworn in, Jack was ecstatic, whispering in his client's hairy ear that he could already hear the jingle of money. Jeeter didn't fully understand, but seemed pleased.

When Jeeter took the stand, the bailiff noted a faint odor of what he later described as rum. Jeeter seemed thrilled with all the attention as he launched into a description of the event for the jury.

"I'se in terrible pain for days and coon't earn ma keep. Arm still pains me terr'ble during a thunder storm. I use ta play th'accordion for friends and fambly, but can't any longer, pains too great in m'elbow. Probl'y never play for my grand childrens."

The stern demeanor of Judge Benson did little to offset the theatrics Jack had managed to elicit from his well-tutored client. The defense noted on cross-examination, however, that Jeeter wasn't married and didn't have children or grandchildren, but the jury didn't seem concerned about this detail.

"Rear tire on my truck'd gone flat on me in the middle the night and I'd ta blow it up 'afore I went back to the lumber mill where I'se workin'. Probl'y shoon't say "blow it up," 'cause that's jess what happened. I had to reflate it. I had a 'pressor I made myself and put the hose on it and let 'er begin to fill while I drank some coffee outta my thermos. Next thing I knew, the tire'd 'sploded and my arm was hangin on me like a horse's dick. Couldn't move it or nothin'."

Gavel down from the bench… "Mr. Tyler, please ask your client to confine his remarks to what happened and leave out his graphic descriptions!"

"Yes, your honor," answered Jack, nodding to Jeeter.

Mr. Levy rose for cross-examination.

"Mr. Parenteau, you have told us you want to play an accordion for your grandchildren and yet you have neither accordion nor grandchildren. You must know that truck tires can only be safely inflated inside a steel cage for the very reason that caused your injury. When you connected your homemade compressor to the tire, did you have a pressure valve preset to the proper inflation pressure? Do you know what the proper pressure for that size tire is? Why didn't you inflate it inside a tire cage like the safety warnings say you must? Had you been drinking when you inflated the tire?

Jeeter stared open-mouthed at his lawyer.

"Answer the questions Mr. Parenteau," Judge Benson ordered.

"I always filled my tires right. I know when they'se full 'cause the sags gone and I don't have no cage 'cept for my dog, Rooter. How's I s'posed to know the tire's gonna go all wild on me and break my arm in three places?"

Gavel down from the bench. "Just answer the questions as they are asked Mr. Parenteau and try and control your theatrics."

Testimony continued throughout the afternoon until Judge Benton ordered a recess at 5 P.M. Summary arguments began at 9 A.M. the following morning. Jack painted a rather bleak picture of his client's poverty, lack of education, and intermittent employment, as Jeeter nodded vigorously by his side.

"'Sides that," Jeeter interrupted, "I don't even have indoor plumbings since the pipes froze up and burst on me."

Gavel down from the bench. "Mr. Tyler, if you cannot control your client, I'll have him removed from the proceedings."

"We understand your honor," Jack responded and then leaned over to admonish Jeeter, who appeared hurt.

Mr. Levy showed examples of his employer's efforts to ensure the safe inflation of truck tires, printed information on tire sizes, pressures, and safe inflation procedures.

After summation, Jack assessed the collective demeanor of the jury and was convinced that his client's tale of pain and suffering played better with them than did the defendant's technical exegesis on safe tire inflation techniques. Besides, he'd made sure that the jury understood in his summation that Jeeter could read little beyond his name, some can labels, and a few road signs.

The jury's first order of business was to select a foreman and they chose Mildred Smith. Millie was a retired English teacher and the current president of the local grange. She was known for her common sense, organized thinking, and plain speaking. Besides, many on the jury had had her as a high school English teacher, so she was elected without dissent.

Millie polled the jury to get a sense of how they were leaning. She was not surprised to find that her peers were almost to a person sympathetic to the plaintiff's tale of suffering at the hands of a faceless Ohio tire company. Millie kept her objections to herself. She had not been swayed by Jeeter's theatrics and saw through Jack Tyler's courtroom antics. Had Jeeter learned to read, this might not have happened and it wasn't the tire company's fault that Jeeter dropped out in fifth grade. She agreed with Mr. Levy that the tire company had done its best to ensure safe use of their tires. She also knew it was a losing battle, trying to convince her peers, and so she made a couple of points about Jeeter's checkered history and the well-known fact that his morning coffee would fuel a chainsaw.

Knowing she would never sway the decision in favor of Firestone, she reminded the jury that they were also obliged to set a fair monetary award appropriate to the damages suffered. No one on the jury disagreed with Millie on this point. She asked the bailiff for an adding machine and the work of adding up Jeeter's losses began.

At 3:45 P.M., Millie informed the bailiff that the jury had reached a decision. The proceedings were called to order and the jury filed back in.

Jack Tyler sat slumped in his chair, grinning like a fox. Jeeter sat slumped in his chair breathing fumes that would have ignited if smoking were allowed in the courtroom. Mr. Levy sat slumped in his chair fearing a very bad outcome for his company.

"All rise," said the bailiff. Jack had to pull his client to his feet and hold him upright with a hand under his armpit.

"Has the jury reached a verdict?" intoned Judge Benson.

"We have your honor," answered Millie.

"And how did you find in the case of Parenteau v. Firestone Tire and Rubber?"

"We found in favor of the plaintiff, you Honor."

Jack Tyler drove his right fist into his left hand, but made no noise.

Jeeter looked quizzically at the man holding him up.

Tom Levy stared at the floor as if the outcome had been pre-ordained and dreaded informing his company of another massive liability settlement against them.

Showing no emotion, Judge Benson asked Millie if the jury had settled on a monetary award.

"We have your honor."

"And what might that amount be, Madam Foreman?"

"Four thousand, four hundred and eight-four dollars, your Honor."

All heads looked up in astonishment. Jack shook his head sideways as if he had misheard. Tom Levy looked up suddenly, grinning from ear-to-ear, and Jeeter let out a triumphant holler, followed by a series of hoots.

"We won, Jeesum crow, you done it, like you said. Never heer'd 'a so much money. Yeehaw!"

He withdrew a pint of screech from the inside vest pocket of his greasy suit jacket and thrust the bottle at Jack who was still non-plussed. Jeeter then spun around and gave him a bear hug that showered Jack with liquor.

"Bailiff, please remove Mr. Parenteau from the courtroom until he recovers," Judge Benson pronounced. Millie tried to hide a smile, but did not miss Judge Benson's arch wink.

Judge Benson thanked the jury for their deliberations and "their commitment to justice well served."

Lila's Bucket

HARDWOOD FLATS DOES not appear on most local maps but the name is used by locals to describe an unmarked space between Elmore, Wolcott, and Worcester. It is a hardscrabble bog of isolated ponds, marshland, and mixed second-growth hardwoods and occasional stands of young evergreens. Walking in the woods one can always hear running water somewhere. Much of its terrain seems to float on an inland sea. Here and there, a few dirt roads, passable except in mud season, wind through the woods, feeding into corduroyed logging roads and then tapering off into hunting trails and deeryards. Occasional year-round dwellings nestle here and there on the passable roads. Hunters or hikers will occasionally run across abandoned farmhouses mouldering in clearings marked by their overgrown lilac bushes or unpruned apple trees. Further in, they may encounter a tarpaper deer camp with sun-bleached antler racks over a padlocked door.

Lila and her husband, Theron, have lived most of their lives in the Flats, coming out occasionally to the Elmore Store to "trade" for necessities. Lila is 91 and Theron 93. Lila didn't get "the sugar" early like her girlfriend Flo, who suffers from terrible dropsy. Lila was diagnosed at 87. Except for a few skin cancers and a locked-up shoulder, Theron has kept his health. He grows cut flowers and root vegetables to sell at the Morrisville farmer's market or to aging hippies who sometimes come to their ramshackled house to buy them right out of Theron's stone-lined root cellar where they are available year-round.

Rena LeClaire, the Morristown home health nurse, had been troubled for some time over Theron's steadfast rejection of her services. She took great pride in the home-based care she provided for the town's senior citizens. Last year, Rena was cited by the County for her "conscientious service" to seniors living at home. It was suggested by some that she contributed to the economic demise of Copley Manor, the town home for dependent seniors.

Much to Rena's dismay, Theron rejected Rena's services outright. Theron told her he "din' wann 'er snoopin' roun' his house lookin' for vi-lations an' the loik." Rena was not accustomed to such out and out rejection. Occasionally, she encountered reticence on the part of a senior or family member that she attributed to modesty, Yankee independence, or pride, but she usually prevailed, patiently explaining that she is only there to help out and doing so only to the extent that her charge permitted. Most of the seniors on her route came to look forward to her ministrations and her company. She brought the mail, a clutch of local gossip, and light groceries if called in advance. While there, she changed bed linens, ran a load of wash if there was a machine, discarded old food, bathed those in her care, and with great authority checked their vitals. One of Rena's charges, who was hard of hearing and kept the hearing aid she brought him in the icebox "so the batt'ries doan run down, would hear "vittles" and insist that he had plenty to eat, then let her check his pulse and blood pressure.

Lila's diabetes progressed very quickly. She is a large woman, but not loosely fat like today's pale-fleshed girls. She'd always been heavy, but the weight that collected over the years like a retirement plan was evenly muscled by the steady routine of chores and helping Theron with the endless gardens and homemade greenhouses that sprung up here and there on their twelve acres. Eventually word went round that a diabetic stroke had left her incapable of speech and partially paralyzed.

This bit of news heightened considerably Rena's sense of urgency about Lila. She suspected things were not right in their home and that Theron had sinister reasons for denying her access to Lila.

She started up her rusty Subaru wagon and headed up Route 12 towards Elmore, turning off just north of the lake and bouncing along the Flats Road until the turnoff that led deep into the puckerbrush and finally to Theron and Lila's homestead. She pulled up into the dirt driveway, set the parking brake, and waited a minute as she always did to give people a chance to gather themselves before she knocked on the door. Theron was just coming in from the woodpile with an armload of biscuit wood for the cook stove. A bright sun shone through the clouds. He spotted Rena and walked purposefully over to the car before she could get out, setting the firewood down hard on the hood of her car and peering into the closed car window. Unable to get out, she rolled down her window and began, "Now see here...."

"No need to git out, y'ain't stayin' and I ain' visitin'. We'se doin' foin w'outcha."

"Theron, I am not here to see you. I come here to see Lila. She's a sick woman and it's my job to take care of her and see to it that she gets medical care."

"She's been to th'ospiddle. They sen' her home and told me ta care for her and I do."

"You can't. You don't know how. She's diabetic. Lila needs special care."

"I give's her sugar med-cin and see's to her. Now git."

"Theron, I don't know what-cher hiding, but I am coming back with the sheriff."

"Bes' bring two, ya old bitch. Now git."

Rena drove off down the dirt road, her chin high and her hands tight on the steering wheel, which seemed to have a mind of its own in the muddy ruts of the thawing road.

Something was not right in that household. The more Rena thought on it, the more her instincts told her Theron was hiding something to do with Lila. Folks often resisted the idea of someone from outside "doing for them." Even after seven years, Rena herself still spent a good hour tidying up her own modest home before Vi, her cleaning lady, came to redo the same. Rena did not want it bruited about the community that she kept an untidy home, and Vi was a gossip.

Theron's overt hostility clearly indicated to Rena that he was hiding something. She had seen enough in her lifetime of service to suspect men who were secretive, and to fear that physical abuse might be the reason. Occasionally, the fatigue and resentment of caring for someone day in and day out could erupt into abuse. Rena remembered that sometime back, Theron had had a run-in with the game warden for jacking deer on his own property. He claimed that he and Lila needed the meat. The confrontation escalated into a tussle after which the warden sported a black eye. No charges were ever brought and Theron was more discreet thereafter. But clearly Theron had it in him to strike out.

She drove straight to Willard Sanders's office. Willard ran the county social welfare office in Morristown. Before these services were consolidated in Montpelier, Willard had been the Overseer of the Poor, an office charged with caring for those unable to provide for themselves within the town. Willard was known as a fair man. One couldn't put one over on Mr. Sanders. He could easily distinguish sloth from need and was not afraid to do so. But he also understood the stress and indignity that poverty placed on families. It was in his nature to treat those in his care with great respect, and he made sure that Rena did as well. His father's sister had died young in the county poor farm.

Thursday afternoons at four, Rena reported to him on her service visits, noting any changes in health, family problems, or household issues. Sometimes folks ran out of wood before winter ran out of cold or well lines froze up leaving people without water. In time, their charges either died quietly at home or came to the hospital to die.

It took Willard several minutes to calm Rena down. By this time, Rena had worked up a pretty strong case that Lila was at risk. Theron's rabid behavior when Rena tried to see Lila made clear that something not right was happening in that household. Lila might be the victim of this crazy old goat, she exclaimed. Willard listened calmly to Rena, asked a few questions and promised to follow up with a visit of his own the following day. This did little to calm Rena and she urged that they return together immediately to rescue Lila.

"Theron and Lila have survived seventy years together. Another day is not going to make a difference," said Willard with calm finality.

Rena left shaking her head. After a reheated meatloaf supper, she checked her four-party line and, finding an interlude after a few tries, began dialing her network of chatty friends to try to garner support for her assessment of the danger Lila was in. "Willard's going up tomorrow. Won't take me, thinks it may be too dangerous," she told Gert, a nurse friend of hers who lived in Morristown Corners. "She may be blind now, God knows, stroke left her part paralyzed. The old fool probably doesn't even know she needs a special diet. Probably feeds her candy bars. Even if he don't 'buse her, he's probably killing her out of ignorance. It just troubles me. He won't let me near the house. He's hiding sumpin'. I know it."

The next day the sun burned through the morning clouds by 10 o'clock and the sky was radiant blue. The air was still crisp, but spring was definitely in the air. Sugarmakers were hard it, driving their teams through the woods collecting sap in the big sledge-mounted galvanized tanks.

Willard started up to the Flats in his Plymouth, trying to reconcile Rena's urgent report with the little he knew of Theron and Lila. The couple had never asked for help from his office and, as far as he knew, kept a modest household supported by the sale of Theron's root vegetables and cut flowers. Willard had not seen Lila for a good twenty years and, even then, only on the rare occasions when they came to Graves's Hardware or Gillen's Department Store.

Although determined to get to the bottom of Rena's report, Willard felt little apprehension as he followed the rutted roads deeper into Hardwood Flats. The sun was blazing down as the road wound into the endless stand of boggy alders and the rich smell of earth melting and water running again lifted his spirits. It had been a long winter.

Rena had written down the directions to Theron's farmstead, as there were no accurate maps of the area, divided as it was between the three towns. Willard remembered hunting here as a kid with his friend Eddy Kitonis and getting lost, finally finding their way to a large fire in a nearby logging camp at dusk, having to spend the night there, and following a new road out to Elmore the following morning.

Willard did not pull into Theron's yard, but drove further down the road, parked, and walked back to Theron's. He climbed the uneven cinderblock steps to the steeply tilted porch and knocked on the screen door. He heard footsteps inside and Theron came to the door.

"'Tchwant?" asked Theron, "Veggies? Flowers won' be ready fer 'nother six weeks."

"My name is Willard Sanders and I came to inquire about how you and Lila are getting along," said Willard, looking Theron square in the eye.

"Good enough," allowed Theron. "That nosey bitch Rena send ya?"

"No, I come on my own," said Willard gently. "It's been a long, cold winter and some folk is jus' havin' a hard time of it and I been checkin' on a few of 'em."

"You from that newfangled church what haunts people wi' their home preachin'?"

"No, I come from town, and my job is just to see to folks. How you and Lila doin'? I know Lila suffers from the sugar."

Willard's calm tone of voice and willingness to look Theron in the eye seemed to allay somewhat his suspicion of the stranger and he asked Willard in off the porch. He pointed to a rocker next to the big Glenwood cookstove and slid the enameled coffeepot left so it was directly over the firebox. Willard settled in and was comfortable with the long silence.

"Jes' tell me what you wanna know and don't beat 'round the bush," said Theron quietly, setting a mug of black coffee and a mayonnaise jar full of sugar in front of Willard on the cooler edge of the stove.

"I heard Lila suffered a stroke and it must be hard caring for her. Can she walk around? Did she lose her speech?"

"We make do well 'nuff. She can't walk, shuffles a bit, but I got's ta hole' her up. Sh' let's me know how she's feelin' by smilin' or frownin'. Tha's 'bout it since she suffered the sugar shock."

"When you tend your greenhouses and gardens, does she stay in the house alone?" Willard asked stirring some sugar into his coffee and looking up at Theron.

"I put 'er in the bucket," answered Theron sipping his own coffee.

"The bucket?" asked Willard.

"The bucket," answered Theron.

"I don't understand," said Willard.

"The bucket on my tractor. C'mere. I'll show ya."

Willard rose to follow Theron out the back door toward a ragtag array of greenhouses made out of scavenged windows and lumber. Near a cold frame was parked an old narrow-front-end Allis-Chalmers with a bucket loader suspended by its hydraulics about four feet off the boggy ground. It was wrapped entirely in an old tarp and tied neatly with bailing twine. Theron untied the tarp and pulled it away, folding it and putting it on the tractor seat. Carefully arranged in the bucket loader lay an old mattress on a thick bed of dry hay. There were a couple of old couch pillows at each end.

"I rigged this up for Lila cause she likes to be with me when I'se workin'. I lay's 'er down on the porch and roll 'er onta the mattress, then cover 'er up with her momma's quilt and some feather pilla's. I get's 'er comf'table and she smiles. I know she loikes it. I use these old straps to make sure she don' fall out when she shifts 'roun'. Then I liffs 'er up high and drive 'er to wherever I'se workin'.... sometimes the garden, sometimes the greenhouse or the root cellar." She loikes being where I'se at."

Willard just stared at the contraption. "Looks mighty comfortable to me," he allowed.

"T'is. I tried it m'self. After awhile, Lila'll doze off in the sun and I wake's 'er wi' my special homemade tomata juice she loikes so much. Weather's nice like today, we have lunch where I'se workin'."

"I know you're a busy man, Theron, and spring's surely coming, so I'll be on my way. If you ever need anything, please call on me. "

"No phone, but I can get them ol' hippies down the road to call. Thanks for comin'. Try ta keep that bitch Rena from comin'. She's allus lookin' fer trouble, e'en if there ain' none to be had."

"I will," promised Willard.

Lila's Death

WHEN THERON BROUGHT Lila into the hospital, he knew she was dying, though little had changed since yesterday when she was lying in the tractor bucket watching him as he picked wild apples. It was cool and he'd wrapped her in an extra Johnson Woolen Mill plaid blanket and tied a knit scarf around her head. She smiled as she watched her husband filling bushel baskets with green rust-dappled apples he would later use to make the sour jelly sweetened with maple syrup that she so liked.

After Theron heaved the second basket up onto the small wooden wagon attached to the back of the tractor, he unscrewed his dented thermos and poured Lila a cup of the hot chicken broth he'd made the day before from a spent hen he saw no reason to feed through the winter.

"Warm enough, Honey?" he asked Lila as he brought the dented enamel cup to her lips. Theron understood that his wife couldn't respond but he'd always seen answers in her eyes. It might be a twinkle, frown, or the hint of a smile that he heard as clearly as anything she might have said. Having suffered for several years from "the sugar," Lila had had a diabetic stroke 14 months earlier that left her unable to speak and partially paralyzed. A few months later, Doctor Phil had had to remove several toes on her left foot. Theron, now 93, provided for them both with his various garden projects and the modest social security check they received each month.

It was clear as he placed his hand on her forehead that Lila was cold. She sipped a bit of the chicken broth, but most ran out the side of her lips onto the feather pillow in the tractor bucket. Theron knew something was amiss. He started up the tractor, and headed for home with two bushels of wild apples and an empty basket.

He raised the front loader until it was flush with the porch floor and drove right up against the front porch steps. He then hit the kill-switch on the old International B, climbed the steps, and gathered Lila to him in her quilt and blanket, pulling her gently into the warm kitchen. He fed three maple splits into the cookstove through the large top burner and lifted Lila up onto the daybed near the stove. He saw her wince as he lay her down.

"Y'okay honey?" he asked, noticing a wrinkle in her brow and a tremor in her left hand as he tucked the blanket around her.

He saw the fear in her eyes and again offered her some broth, but she inclined her head away. He worried how scary it would be to be trapped inside a body that could not respond to the commands of its tenant and he sometimes imagined his wife of 72 years as a prisoner in her body. Initially, her stroke had not prevented them from enjoying their time together or even from communicating with expressions of delight, surprise, or dismay.

Theron knew Lila had taken a turn for the worse and determined to wait till the next day to take her to the hospital so as not to importune the doctors and nurses who would be leaving to go home to their own families at this late hour.

The following morning on the trip from Hardwood Flats to Morrisville's Copley Hospital, Lila seemed listless. Her eyes were closed and her head bobbed against the window as Theron made his way slowly along the dirt road leading to Route 12. When they arrived, Theron went in the main entrance and asked for help bringing his wife inside. He was directed to the Emergency entrance around back where an orderly and a nurse pushing a wheelchair were already waiting. Theron and the orderly settled Lila into the wheelchair, but only Theron saw the grimace on her lips and the fear in her eyes as she looked at him. Lila was put in the same room she had recovered in after her "shock" and then again when Dr. Phil amputated three of her toes.

Never taking his eyes off of Lila's face, Theron stood by and held her hand as they waited for Dr. Phil. He could see the fear in her eyes and the occasional glimmers of gratitude for his presence as he held her hand. Only once did he look away, when he heard Doctor Phil enter the room.

"How's our Lila today?' he asked in his familiar bedside manner. Theron saw a wisp of a smile appear on her face. Dr. Phil ordered a round of blood and urine tests and looked carefully at Lila's feet. A nurse joined him and began taking a blood sample.

"I'm going to have to catheterize Lila," Doctor Phil said to Theron and then asked the nurse to "get on it as soon as she finished drawing blood."

Theron looked at Lila and, although he had seen a wide spectrum of fears in his wife's eyes, he had never before seen terror. He abruptly interrupted Dr. Phil.

"We'se not going to do all 'em things, Doc," Theron said, to the surprise of the nurse and Doctor Phil.

"If it's time for Lila to go, we ain't gonna make it harder for her by pokin' her wi' needles and tappin' her like a sugar maple. You give 'er sompin' to make her comf'table and I'se gonna stay here 'n hold 'er hand. Now, git 'less I call ya."

"But Theron, we don't know how sick she is and won't know unless I take some tests. You wouldn't want her leaving you before she's ready."

"She's ready. She told me so."

"But she hasn't spoken in 14 months. How do you know for sure?"

"She talks to me wi' her eyes and it's clear."

A look of relief flooded Lila's face and a hint of a smile appeared.

"See here," Theron said. "She's relieved. I can tell."

The nurse left and shortly returned with a hypodermic needle. Lila looked agitated when she saw the needle. She rolled back Lila's flannel shirt, held her arm firmly and administered the shot quickly.

"You best be gentle wi' my woman. She's been good to me all 'ese years," Theron warned.

"Sometimes it's best to give shots quickly before the patient knows what's happening and tenses the muscle, only makes it hurt more. Martha's a professional. I trusted her with my mother when she was dying... a good nurse."

"That's good Doc, I trust you, if'n you say so. You'se always been good to Lila and me, and fair 'n all. I jes' don't want Lila all agitated when you and I both know she's leavin' us."

"I understand, Theron. You been good to her all these years, I know that. I'm gonna leave you two to one another tonight and we'll see how Lila's faring in the morning. Then we can talk about making her comfortable and whether or not to take some tests to determine how bad her sugar is. I suspect her kidney's failing.

"Martha, can you let the Millie know that Theron will be staying in here with Lila tonight. Theron, I'll see you in the morning. You get some sleep, hear?"

Doctor Phil and Martha left the room. Theron looked back at Lila. She was sleeping peacefully, but breathing erratically.

"Don' know what they gave ya, but ya sure look peaceful. Sleep well. I'll be right here with ya."

Theron pulled a folding chair over by Lila's bedside and sat down. After shooing away a candy striper adamant about serving Lila a small plate containing nothing Theron could recognize, he too fell asleep, holding Lila's hand.

He awoke around 4:30 as it was getting dark. Lila's hand felt cooler and he massaged it gently. She opened her eyes and smiled to see him.

He brushed a wisp of hair away from her eyes and patted her cheek. The clear skin that had so entranced him as a young man was still clear, but had aged to a pale parchment under which he could see bluish arteries. The eyes that had so sparkled with light and excitement when Theron brought Lila home for the first time to his modest farm on the Flats were viscous and yellowed now with the years they had accrued together.

"You been cryin' Honey? There's no need. I'se right here and ain't goin' nowheres."

He again saw a faint glimmer of a smile as he looked into the eyes that for months had taken up the work of her mouth and lips, now silenced by stroke.

Around 6:30, Martha returned to give Lila another shot and, under the watchful eyes of Theron she proceeded very gently, rolling back Lila's sleeve and gently massaging her forearm before inserting the needle.

"Can you tell 'em we don' want no food," asked Theron.

"Yes, I will," Martha answered. "Sure you don't want a plate for yourself?"

"I'd take an apple if you have one, but I ain't hungry beyond that."

"One apple comin' up. They're fresh in from the Kitonis orchard up yer way."

"Jerry grows good apples," Theron said as Martha left the room and closed the door behind her.

Theron pulled the chair up to the bed and watched Lila as she again fell into a deep sleep.

Theron drifted into memories of their times together as a young couple, working to make their way. They had no neighbors on whom they could depend and often talked at suppertime about what they could raise for sale, what they would need to trade for in town, and what they could grow in the short growing season on their hardscrabble land. They owned enough land but much of it was forested, although Theron had clear-cut, and removed stones and tree roots from several acres for gardens, orchards, and berry patches. Higher up in the woods he dug blackberry canes, ginseng, and small apple trees to transplant into his new fields.

In the early years, he often joked with Lila about finding a recipe for the crop of stones heaved up by frost each spring in his fields. Just when he thought he had finally rid one of his gardens of the stones and boulders, his horse-drawn plow would hit a stone and Sadie would know to stop while Theron took out his steel pry bars and levered the stone out of the ground. Ones smaller than a turkey, he'd lug over and toss on the rubble wall which grew higher each year with his new harvest of stones. If it was "only the tit of an iceberg," as he liked to say, he'd fetch a shovel, dig all around it until he could get a rope around it and then unhook the plow and hitch Sadie up to the ropes and urge her on while he worked the stone from behind with a crowbar until he levered it free and it rolled up onto the surface.

Then he'd unhitch Sadie from the stone and together they'd walk back to the shed to get the stone-boat he'd made with some hornbeam, a piece of steel, and section of log chain. Once he got the boulder up onto the stone-boat, Sadie could easily haul it to the edge of the field.

He remembered how watching Lila toiling in the garden would excite him and how lying in bed at night after supper, the images of her would come back and stir him to touch her. He thought of how the many times they'd made love never brought them the children they both dreamt of raising. The subject was not one talked about with strangers so they'd never sought help, and simply contented themselves with one another's company.

Sometime in the night when all the sounds of a busy hospital had quieted, Theron heard — first in a dream and then it woke him — a low moan from Lila. It scared him into a sudden awakening, as he'd heard nothing from her for so long. The noise ended just as suddenly but she, too, was now awake with a fearful look in her eyes.

"What's wrong honey? You okay?"

Her eyes closed slowly and he reached for her hand, the coolness of which surprised him. He pulled the blankets up to her chin and over their held hands.

She seemed to relax somewhat and he wondered if she, too, had been dreaming.

"I wanted to tell you my sorrowfuls," Theron began.

She opened her eyes again.

"I'se sorry for the times I'se away from you, going to town, the time I had to take work at the lumber mill to earn us money for winter stores, the time Pa died and I was gone for so long, the times I spent up on the mountain when I couldn't get the sadness out of me."

He looked into her eyes for a sign of forgiveness.

"I'se sorry for not giving you the children we both wanted. We was never lonely in each other's company, but I know how much we both wanted little children to raise and work together in our gardens. I'se most sorry about that. I could see in your eyes you wantin' little ones, too.

"I'se sorry 'bout the hard winters we spent together. Seems like no matter how hard we worked, some falls we just couldn't put up enough to get through 'em winters and I'd have to take credit in town, which we both promised never to do, 'cause it would get us off wrong come spring.

"I's sorry for my long bout's of sadness and the times I'd go all silent and you'd try so hard to bring me comfort, but I couldn't be comforted no matter, and I'd have to jess get through the sadness by myself, knowing it would go away and you'd be there and not be harsh on me and all. I've always had the sadness in me, but you was always there. You was patient for me.

"I know you could 'a had a better life in town or with someone who done better 'n all, but I did the best I knew to do. Maybe I din't know all the hows and whys of life, but I always loved you best I could in my ways."

The following morning on her rounds, Martha came in at six. Theron was lying next to Lila in the hospital bed holding her hand. Martha found no vital signs in Lila and Theron was breathing peacefully.

Theron woke up when he heard Martha calling out arrangements in the hall. He rose from Lila's side and kissed her slowly on the lips as Dr. Phil entered the room. Martha informed him that Lila had "passed" in the night. Theron said, "No, she died," thanked them both and left, telling Dr. Phil, "take good care of my Lila. I'll be back for her tomorrow."

Lila's Burial

THERON WAS WAITING at the front door of the hospital. He imagined the hospital to be like the few stores at which he traded, opening at 8 A.M. and closing at 5 P.M. So when he saw the clock over the reception desk turn to 8:00, he pushed open the glass door and entered, approaching the desk and said to the volunteer, "I'se here to pick up Lila and bring her home."

The volunteer scanned a clipboard on the side of her desk.

"I am so sorry to tell you sir that Mrs. Walcott died the day before yesterday. Did no one from here manage to reach you?"

"I know she's dead, I was lyin' wi' 'er upstairs when she doied. I'se jess here to take 'er home. Doctor Phil'll know. He here yet?"

"He gets in at nine, but let me call our Social Services Director, Claire Densmore. I'm sure she'll be able to help you."

"No need to trouble 'er. I'll jess wait 'til Doctor Phil comes. Jess tell 'im I'se here waitin' on him. I'll be roight here."

Keeping her eyes on the strange man pacing in the lobby, the volunteer surreptitiously picked up the receiver and called Claire's office down the hall, whispering into the phone about an elderly man pacing in the lobby looking to pick up his deceased wife.

Small rural hospitals manage widely varying admissions and urgencies. They triage and process those in need based on set parameters. But in a rural hospital serving the economic spectrum from well-heeled patients arriving by ambulance from the ski slopes and chalets of Stowe to those arriving in pickups from the tiny hamlets of Eden, Wolcott, Elmore, Belvidere and Waterville, anyone who does not conform to the usual presenting ailments ends up in Claire's office. Over many years, she has learned the diversity of woes that make people sick, believe they're sick, or simply need help: an elderly man dodging his approaching death because he hasn't been able to make living arrangements for his dog after he dies, a widow living in her trailer who first lost her dentures and then her glasses and can't afford to replace either. A multitude of troubles can arise in the hills and hollows of tiny towns where poverty is rife and state and federal relief services are either little understood or suspect.

Claire came into the waiting area and recognized Theron from his time at the hospital when Lila had her stroke and when Doctor Phil had operated on her. Recognizing Claire, Theron agreed to follow her to her office until Doctor Phil showed up.

"Bankers' hours, I guess," Theron muttered. "'Bou' this time I'se thinkin' on lunch. Folks don't seem to know much 'bout work these days," he continued, shaking his head.

"Doctor Phil works hard enough," Claire asserted as they walked down the tiled corridor. "Just last Friday, he was here all night. We had a flurry of folks in and his relief has to come all the way from Burlington. I've seen him work 18 hours without stopping, except for a coffee on the run. Can get mighty busy here, 'specially in the fall and before Christmas."

"I know he's a good man. He took good care of my Lila the two times she was here and he sewed up my hand once and din't charge me nothing, so I brung 'im four quarts a' wild blueberries and a jug a' syrup for his troubles."

Claire settled in behind her desk and Theron alighted in a chair on the other side.

"So you're going to bury your Lila. I am sorry she's gone. Good woman, Lila was."

"Sh' was a good woman and I wanna do roight by 'er in her dying. I'se gonna bury 'er myself in her favorite spot where we use ta have our picnics down by the brook below the berry patches. I saved up some a' ma cut flowers 'n all. I'se gonna treat her roight, like she treated me all 'er loife."

Claire could see the moisture in Theron's eyes.

"Just so you know, let me tell you your choices under the law."

"I don't care 'bout no law. I cares 'bout ma Lila."

"I know that, Theron, but we both want to do this right so there's no trouble like you had with Rena."

"That cow better steer clear a' me and Lila!"

"She won't be anywhere around. Don't worry about Rena."

"Lila can be buried in the Elmore Cemetery or you can now bury her at home. She doesn't have to be embalmed but she must buried within three days of her death if you choose not to. It's not strictly legal to transport a dead person yourself, but I know Doctor Phil and I'd overlook you bringing

Lila home yourself. Doctor. Phil has already filled out the death certificate and necessary papers so we can release Lila to you today, but you have to promise us both that you'll bury her tomorrow wherever you choose and I know you know how to do that."

Theron seemed far away. During her set speech, she noticed his head hanging lower and suddenly his chest heaved with a heavy sob.

"She was such a good woman. Don't know what I'll do without her. She and I'se been together over 70 years and now she's gone. I know sure 'nough how to take care a' myself. I have well 'nough since she had her sugar stroke, but now I don't know's I wanna with her gone and all."

Theron broke down in deep sobs and tried to catch his breath. Claire came around her desk and put her arm on Theron's shoulder as he wept freely into his hands.

After several quiet minutes a knock on the door prompted Theron to pull withdraw his handkerchief from his back pocket, wipe his eyes, and blow his nose.

"Morning Theron, I thought maybe I'd see you yesterday, but we've been taking good care of Lila. I got all her paperwork done and I bet Claire has explained your options to you. She's good at that."

Sensing Theron was not yet ready to talk, Claire explained to Doctor Phil that Theron would be burying Lila himself at home.

"She explained the rules...you can do as you please. I didn't get a chance to say much when you left, but I am truly sorry that Lila's gone."

"Me, too, Doc, terrible sorry. I miss her already."

"I'm sure you do. You'll need to take care of yourself in the next few months, especially with winter comin' on. You all ready, got your wood up and stores in?"

"Mostly," answered Theron blowing his nose again.

Claire phoned an orderly to bring Lila to the emergency room entrance and to help Theron get her into his pickup.

Doctor Phil and Claire waved goodbye to Theron as he drove off with Lila sitting next to him, her torso bound upright to the seat with surgical tape.

Claire took the afternoon to drive out to Hardwood Flats to let a few of Theron's closer neighbors know that Lila had died and ask them to check in on him. The trip was best made in person as few of his neighbors had phones — locals or hippies. They all knew and bought fruit, vegetables and cut flowers from Theron and Lila during the growing season and root cellar vegetables, canned goods, and seasoned firewood during the winter.

When she'd made her rounds, she stopped at Theron's to check in on him. He wasn't there, but Lila lay on her daybed near the cookstove. A freshly made pine box was propped up near the porch window. A milk pail full of cut fresh flowers stood in the corner and large pile of dried flowers lay on the kitchen table. Claire worried that Theron was digging her grave himself.

As she turned to leave, she left an envelope of cash on the counter that she was authorized to dispense for folks in dire need. It was only $40 but would be significant to Theron who bought little more than gas for his truck, tractor, and chainsaw, kerosene for his lamps, spring seeds, flour, cooking oil, salt, sugar, and coffee.

As she stepped off the porch, she saw Theron coming and waved to him. When he reached the porch, he asked Claire, "Wanna see where I'se gonna bury my Lila?"

"I'd like that," Claire answered, and followed Theron down the hill along a fern-lined path through a thicket of ash and hickory to the brook that ran along the east boundary of his property. They soon arrived at a moss-covered slope along the edge of the brook. A wide grave stood on the upper slope surrounded by a profusion of cut daylilies, dahlias, monkshood, black-eyed susans and anemones and a cluster of fruiting chokecherry branches. Among the flowers sat four Mason jars of Theron's venison mincemeat.

"I'se gonna sit wi' 'er tonight and then bring her down in her bucket and lay 'er ta rest tamorrow mornin' when the sun's highest."

"You want any visitors for when you bury Lila?" Claire asked.

"No, I best be alone, not sure I can be civil. Sad, doncha know... overcomes me sometime. Best if I be alone, but thanks for offerin'."

Claire followed Theron back to the house, said her goodbyes and drove back to the hospital where the needs of more folks had piled up in her message box.

Theron spent the night talking with his Lila, reminiscing on their travails and joys together. He held her hand for much of the evening and kept the fire burning as he knew how she had disliked being cold, especially after her stroke.

The next morning, he brought the tractor around to the front and prepared it for her last ride. He shook the dead stink bugs and wasps out of the old mattress, wrapped her in her mother's crazy quilt and fluffed up her feather pillow. He then drove the tractor up to the front porch and brought Lila out and laid her out like he always had in the bucket. Then he propped the pine coffin up on the drag bar and leaned it against the back of the tractor seat and set off down the path to Lila's burial site.

When he arrived, he climbed down and laid out two manila ropes parallel to one another on the ground near the dug grave and set the coffin over them. He then lowered the bucket so he could lift Lila off and lay her in the pine coffin. When he had arranged her comfortably, he set two Mason jars of mincemeat in the coffin on either side of her, placed a bouquet of his darkest dahlias on her breast, kissed her goodbye, and sat down on the moss and wept.

After some time he recovered himself, lifted the coffin cover in place and nailed it shut with twelve finish nails he had in his overalls pocket. He then tied the ropes around the hydraulic arms of the loader, lifted Lila's coffin off the moss, climbed back on the idling tractor, and inched forward until the coffin hung over the newly dug grave. Then he slowly lowered Lila into her grave. He turned off the tractor, dismounted, pulled the ropes out from under the coffin, and sat down on the moss and sobbed.

After several minutes, he thought he heard someone coming down the path and turned to see his old friend, Willard Sanders, limping slowly through the ferns.

"Hello, Theron, thought maybe you could use some company while you laid Lila to her rest. I just heard from Doctor Phil, you was buryin' 'er today, and I thought I'd come see you and say g'bye ta 'er, too, and see how you'se farin'.

"You dig that all by yer lonesome? That's a lot a work for a man yer age. I'm too old now ta help, but I could got you some help."

"I done it okay."

Willard sat down next to Theron and the two talked for some time about the days when they were young and just starting out to make their way in the world.

Finally, Theron got to his feet, gathered up the rest of his flowers and dropped them onto the coffin. With the help of his walking stick, Willard clambered up and stood by as Theron started the tractor and began backfilling the hole he'd dug the day before by hand. He smoothed over the disturbed earth with the back edge of the loader, offered Willard a seat in the bucket and sputtered up the path to home.

Theron survived that lonely winter but died of a heart attack in the spring while cutting wood for a winter he would never see.

Good Fences...

ONE HOT AUGUST day when Leo Barbeau's neighbor, Dee Estey, was bending over trying to attach the driveshaft on her side-delivery rake to the PTO on her International, Leo was so enticed by the vision of her elevated buttocks that he hopped off his Massey Ferguson, over the fence, and had at Dee in a savage rut that brought noisy pleasure to them both - Leo, panting like a race horse at stud and Dee, lowing like a longhorn.

When his prize Hereford bull did the same thing the following week to one of Dee's Holstein heifers, she was furious and let Leo know. His efforts to remind her of their own moment of bliss did nothing to calm her rage at what his bull had done to her heifer. She left a letter in his mailbox telling him in no uncertain terms to castrate, tether, or shoot his bull. Leo was deeply hurt by the tone of the letter.

To add insult to injury, Dee then filed suit in Hyde Park, and Sheriff Art Plouffe served Leo with papers claiming $500 in damages. Leo reluctantly called Will Gilbert, the younger of two local lawyers, to mount his defense. Will enlisted Jake Bedard, the town fence viewer, to survey the abutting fence between Leo and Dee's farms. Jake determined that the barbed wire portion of the boundary fence was indeed adequate, but that the stone rubble wall separating about a third of the two pastures, though legally constituting a fence, was inadequate to prevent the incursion of a determined bull. Jake took two pictures with his new Polaroid in case the suit went to trial.

To the delight of townsfolk, it did, and was to be heard by a circuit rider, Judge "Spike" Dyer. Dee didn't ask for a jury trial since, in her view, it was an open and shut case of bad herd management.

The trial lasted one day during which Leo slouched and pouted in the back of the courtroom, still stung by Dee's hostility. In Leo's defense, Will made the case that, according to an 1879 survey, a portion of the rubble fence was on Dee's property so that responsibility for its maintenance in fact rested with both landowners.

"Ergo," a term left over from his earlier practice in the more urbane courts of Montpelier, "Leo could not be held solely accountable for his bull's errant insemination of Dee's heifer."

Dee's attorney, Clayton Desmets, countered that a 90-year-old survey could hardly be deemed accurate, while grudgingly acknowledging the authority of the fence viewer. He further countered that neither party had knowledge of which section of the fence the fervid bull had transgressed.

At this point, Will moved for a summary judgment in favor of his client, since there was inadequate evidence to find in favor of the plaintiff. Judge Dyer, struggling to maintain judicial temperament, agreed and the case was dismissed.

Even though he won, Leo still looked glum. Dee stormed out of the courtroom without even looking at him. Judge Dyer summoned Leo to the bench, leaned forward, and whispered, "Which portion of the fence did you jump?"

Leo looked at the judge non-plussed but, respectful of his office, answered, "the barbed wire part."

"Better you than me," said Judge Dyer with a broad wink as he left the bench.

Leo and Dee were married in the spring. Leo maintained his Herefords and thrived in the emerging beef market, while Dee assiduously continued her dairy breeding program, eventually winning a Green Pasture Award for most productive herd. Her heifer gave birth to a bob calf that was promptly sold into slaughter and Dee gave birth to a girl the following May.

Parish Secretary

"DR. JOHNSON GAVE me a copy of my X-ray. Take a look. See there? No, no, right here!" Madge said, focusing Father DesLauriers' attention on a speck of light on the film. "Doctor says it's just a mote of dust, but I s'pect it's a baby cancer growing in there. He's got no way ta know really, does he?"

Madge was sustained by her ills. It was believed among her friends that if she didn't have enough things wrong with her, she'd surely die. Her grandfather had been a country doctor and she'd inherited two of his medical texts from her mother. These broadened the panoply of ailments with which she regaled her friends and anyone unwary enough to ask, "How you doing?"

Madge was the parish secretary in Johnson. She had worked for Father DesLauriers for 20 years since he came to town in 1961 to take over the small Catholic parish after Father Rostand retired. The new priest learned quickly never to say a casual, "How are you?" or "How you doin' today Madge?" especially if he had any pressing matters on his mind. It let Madge, who always took the question literally, unleash a bevy of malady descriptions that sometimes turned Father D.'s face beet red while he feigned interest in the details of her female anatomy.

Father D.'s hearing was not as it had been when he was ordained. Once, when Madge whispered to him that she suspected she had a prolapsed uterus and that her vulva might need attention, Father D. had offered to drive her to the dealer in Burlington. Neither Madge nor Father D. was ever able to untangle the confusion, especially when Father D. remembered that Madge drove a Plymouth.

Madge moved on, concentrating on the possibility that she might be having a gout attack. This persisted for several weeks until Dr. Johnson explained to her that gout attacks were limited to the lower extremities and could not be the cause of shooting pains in her neck. Madge, down but not out, soon began to complain of some pain and swelling in her ankles, proving herself right all along.

When Father D. made his semi-annual visit to see Bishop Joyce in Burlington to report on his parish's census of the faithful, its finances, and the number of his pastoral visits, he was caught off guard when, after kissing the Bishop's ring, Bishop Joyce asked after Madge's uterus. Father D., fearing that the Bishop might be inferring an excess of intimacy between him and his secretary, stammered that he thought it was better, making her uterus sound more like a family relative. Bishop Joyce asked Father D. to convey his sincerest sympathy and best wishes for a speedy recovery, which would include a mention in his prayers. Father D. thanked him and assured him that he would convey the message.

When in the office, Madge always answered the parish phone and Father D. was aghast to think she would have importuned the bishop with a digression on her female problems, but he knew that she spared no one the intimate details of her afflictions.

On the drive back on Route 15 along the Lamoille River bottom land with all its verdant farms, Father D. wondered whether to confront Madge about the incident or let it be. The Bishop did not seem upset and, after all, it was his job to solace the afflicted, but on the other hand, he did not want her rattling on to callers about her problems when the caller himself might be in real need. He also did not want to sour their relationship, because when it came to keeping the books and parish records, Madge did a good job.

Gradually, Father D. trained himself to confine his questions to the weather, a topic on which Madge had little to say unless it afflicted her lumbago or the arthritis in her left hip. If she was deprived of the opportunity to retail her afflictions, they would attack and manifest themselves and she would begin to utter pained noises that would elicit a concerned inquiry.

In time, Father D. came to the decision that he would simply have to live with Madge's proclivity but would avoid raising any discussion of health in front of her. The silence had an effect on Madge akin to bubonic plague and new symptoms soon bubbled forth.

The week she determined to suffer from shingles was harder for Father D. than for Madge, as it coincided with his scheduled week as a circuit rider, saying mass and hearing confession in Eden and Hyde Park as well as Johnson, on top of which he had to escort, introduce and orient a new priest from Senegal whose name he couldn't pronounce and who spoke little English but was fluent in Father D.'s native French. Unfortunately, not all parishioners in these small towns, shared Father D.'s French-Canadian background and this would put the new priest at some disadvantage, especially in the confessional.

Every Thursday afternoon, Madge looked forward to hearing a litany of afflictions when Father D. returned from his pastoral visit to parishioners in Copley Hospital or in the Pine Haven Rest Home where nine elderly parishioners were living out their last days. She would listen intently and then compare unfavorably the sufferings of the ailing and aging parishioners with her own, which often took up their entire tea break and much of the rest of the afternoon. In an effort to recapture his Thursday afternoons from a recitation of the comparative ills of his ailing flock and those of his parish secretary, Father D. rescheduled the visitation to the afternoon and went straight home to the rectory after completing his rounds.

This was the last straw and Madge came down with psoriasis. Although she was unable to show any overt symptoms, she explained to all who would listen that she had a latent version that would lie low and haunt her health for years and then suddenly when she was under stress manifest itself in an outbreak of suppurating carbuncles that would make it impossible for her to ever appear in public again. Father D. expressed his sympathy, grateful that the psoriasis had eclipsed further discussion of her menopausal symptoms.

Late that fall, Father D. went in for his annual physical and learned that his years of smoking had taken their toll, as his mother had suggested they would, even though he had managed to quit nine years ago on his fiftieth birthday. A subsequent chest x-ray showed an inoperable blizzard of malignancy in his left lung and incipient cancer in his right lung. A biopsy confirmed the diagnosis and Father D. began to prepare himself to meet the God he had served faithfully since he was 23.

For the first month, he kept the information to himself but, as his consultations gave greater intimations of his mortality, he wrote his mother in Quebec and his younger sister in upstate New York to tell them. He also sent a letter to Bishop Joyce so that he might plan ahead for whatever assistance Father D. might need as his pastoral capacity ebbed.

The only person he dreaded telling was Madge, perhaps for fear that she would appropriate his disease or, at the very least, feel a need to compete. This feeling of resentment towards the woman with whom he had worked for so long took him wholly by surprise. Antipathy was generally alien to Father D., one of the reasons he was so loved by his parishioners. After applying some serious prayer to the issue, he resolved to persist in his vocation until the Lord no longer gave him the strength to continue.

Parish work always accelerated in the Advent season and Madge's medical digressions appeared to diminish as her workload increased. As Father D. himself labored harder to breathe, he began to think more about the woman who had worked so hard alongside him and began to wonder what deep sadness or loneliness within her had inspired such a rich invention of troubles.

As his coughing got worse and his white handkerchief began to show flecks of blood, Madge finally confronted him and asked what was wrong. Father D. told her in two declarative sentences, the first one, his diagnosis; the second, his prognosis.

"Why didn't you tell me?" she cried out, bursting into tears. "You should have told me."

"It's God's will. My work here will be done soon. There's nothing to be sad about. Let us finish our work here together well," he said, giving her a kiss on the forehead and drying the tears running down her cheeks a tissue.

When he thought about it later that night in the rectory as he had his single dram of brandy and finished reading his breviary before retiring, it came to him what Madge had been asking for, probably since she was a little girl. She had not gotten it from her hard-bitten mother who had raised her children during the Depression years, several of which were spent at the county poor farm. She had certainly not gotten it from her abusive father who disappeared when she was fourteen, nor, he now realized, had she gotten it from the man of God for whom she had worked so hard. Father D., pouring himself another drink, suddenly teared up, overwhelmed by his own sin of omission.

After celebrating Christmas with his parishioners, Father D. said his good-byes to one and all. He died on Ash Wednesday.

After his death, Madge's complaints vanished. But in their place came a true affliction, though only after she had retired on a modest pension.

Slowly it became apparent that Alzheimer's had taken hold.

She and Father Foluke, Father D.'s successor, had become good friends. When he came to visit her as she retreated further into her dementia, he would greet her warmly and ask how she was.

"Never better!" Madge would let forth. "I feel great, but I have to tell you, it ain't easy working with these spent hens, always complaining about this and that and, of course, half of 'em are crazy as loons, don't 'cha know. I tell you, it's truly the Lord's work and I'm just grateful he's given me the patience to stay at this job. It ain't easy, I tell you."

Father Feluke would smile, give her his blessing, and leave.

Heavy Equipment

PETE'S OBSESSION WITH heavy equipment included earthmoving equipment, though he could hardly afford to own any. He "owned" a skidder that he'd found abandoned in the woods and rebuilt. He was also working on an old D-6 dozer that someone had dropped off for repair and then died. Since it was not expressly mentioned in the customer's last "will and testicle" when it was read in "prostate court," as Pete told his friend Duke, he understood the dozer now belonged to him.

After the owner was safely buried, Pete snuck up to his mobile home in Eden to see if he could find some of the missing parts, and, sure enough, he found the small donkey engine that was used to start the diesel and a few other critical parts like an extra set of cutting blade angle cylinders and some track bearings. As he poked around the yard further, he was surprised that someone as badly off as the resident of the trailer might have even had a 20-year-old, broken bulldozer, unless, of course, he'd stolen it. It was clear to Pete from the free-standing porcelain toilet in the front yard that smelled of recent use that the deceased was not well-off.

Pete loaded the dozer parts into his truck, along with a set of open-ended wrenches and a logging chain he found lying on the ground and made tracks for home.

A retiring dentist from Quebec City named Ti-Jean Ardoin bought the six-acre parcel abutting Pete's property. Pete had had his eye on it since it was first listed, but had not saved enough from his meager earnings to make even an insulting offer. But he was in no particular rush, as he felt comfortable using as his own any adjoining property not expressly lived on by someone else. For some time he'd been harvesting wood for his woodstove and collecting stone for his root cellar from the property without any notice or complaint.

The previous owner knew Pete wanted the land and was willing to make some concession, but it was still well beyond Pete's means. He had hoped to sell the skidder to raise enough to augment his offer, but the new buyer made a cash offer too close to the asking price to ignore and the deal concluded within two weeks. Pete was dismayed and decided simply to plant the new owner and whatever he might build out of existence.

The new owner's view of the Mansfield Range was over Pete's property, so any effort by Pete to plant his new neighbor out of view would also eclipse his view of the mountain, which had been a primary incentive for Dr. Ardoin's purchase of that particular parcel.

Unlike Ardoin, Pete's assessment of property value was based on the quality of the woodlot, its water source, and the distance to the nearest neighbor. He often told Duke, "If you can't piss out your own front door or have a good rut on the front lawn, don't buy it!" By this standard, his own property had just been considerably devalued, so he transplanted a tight row of fast-growing popples along the new boundary.

Dr. Ardoin didn't begin construction of his dream retirement home until spring of the following year at which point the trees were already tickling his view. When he met with the contractor to lay out plans for the picture windows that would bring the celebrated view into his living room he noticed the wall of poplars and decided to have them removed.

Site excavation began in late May when the clay soil had dried out enough for an excavator to begin digging. A concrete crew followed with prefab forms and then a pumper truck filled them to form a foundation. Pete's evening inspections, after the workers quit, astounded him at the sheer size of the dwelling under construction. The foundation footprint was a good 1600 square feet.

As the house rose, Pete kept track of each development. When the framing was done and the roofers were sheathing the roof frame, the windows were delivered and Pete saw the amount of glass going in on the west side of the house. He wondered how his new neighbor planned to heat the place. He figured Ardoin would need to clear-cut his six acres the first year just to get enough wood to heat the place.

Once Pete's inherited dozer was running, he began working for the town on Wednesday and Saturday afternoons plowing under new deposits at the town dump. One Wednesday evening, he returned home to find his poplars all lying on the ground. Whoever did it, violated Pete's first rule of forestry, never cut down a second tree until you've limbed and cut up the first. A random pile of popples lay on the ground where they'd been felled amidst a protrusion of stumps.

Pete was enraged and started over to yell at his new neighbor who was still in Quebec City making arrangements to sell his apartment there. Ignorant of property lines in general, when Pete dug in the new poplars it hadn't occurred to him to check which side he planted them on and he had planted them on his new neighbor's property.

This still didn't give Ardoin any right to cut his trees he reasoned and he saw this as a declaration of war. After railing at Duke, the local sheriff, he decided to plant a new line of popples on his own side of the property line. He chose the tallest he could find on his and his new neighbor's property to transplant.

Dr. Ardoin's new house began to take shape and, after each evening's inspection, Pete kept up a running discussion with himself about his new neighbor's poor judgment. Pete had not seen a house constructed close-up since he built his own 27 years ago and was amazed at how it all came together in pre-made parts, from the concrete forms to the roof trusses and prefab windows. The crowning achievement was a prefab front-door jamb, complete with a glazed oval glass insert, brass hinges, lock hardware, and three keys. Pete took this opportunity to grab a key for safe-keeping.

As interested as he was in the process, the end result still galled him. It looked to him like those tacky houses on the outskirts of Montreal with their gaudy front doors hanging in mid-air and mixed sidings of Z-brick veneer and vinyl shingles. The only thing missing he told his friend Duke was the bathtub Madonna half-buried in the front lawn. The idea of looking at this monstrosity for years to come annoyed Pete.

"Makes my eyes bleed," he told Duke, whom he occasionally consulted on legal matters.

When Doctor Ardoin finally moved in the following spring, an acre of land around his house had been clear-cut and seeded for lawn. Workers installed a four-foot high concrete fountain with "some naked hootchie-kootchie girl dancing in a sprinkle of water," Pete told Duke, "Ugly as mortal sin itself... made me think of the scoot shows in Tunbridge."

Another team arrived and installed boxwood foundation plantings around the split-level house and then laid out some red bark-mulch islands around the property and planted flowering crab apples. When the moving van showed up and started unloading Ardoin's household goods, Pete watched through the scope on his 30.06 from the safety of his woodshed. The next day, he described the furnishings to Duke, wondering how it all fit.

"He's got a dinner table that's all glass, bigger than his picture window, wouldn't want eat off'in that when it's twenty below in there." Duke nodded in agreement.

"You never know with these city folk, what they'se thinking," opined Duke over his coffee. He could sense the bile rising in his friend's gorge and warned Pete to let his new neighbor be.

Several days later, Dr. Ardoin, himself, arrived in a Lincoln Mark III, towing a power boat longer than the car. This was the first Pete had seen of the diminutive Quebecker. Pete owned a trapper boat he poled or rowed around through swamp to set and check his beaver traps, but he'd never seen a boat like the one Ardoin towed into his yard. It had a 100-horse-power Mercury outboard motor, a mahogany front deck and a chrome steering wheel. Pete had seen pictures of these boats but had never seen one close up. Most places Pete fished or trapped wouldn't even be deep enough to float "the destroyer" as Pete christened it. Besides how could one fish with a motor like that...blend any largemouth into soup!

Apart from maintaining the town dump, Pete's diligence and his dozer brought more town work his way. He teamed up with Mac Wilder, who owned a gravel pit and a 12-yard dump truck to bid on the re-grading and crowning of 18 miles of dirt roads connecting Wolcott, Hardwick, and Greensboro. Pete also had yet to get in his wood supply for the following year and dig out and replace the spring box on his property that had silted up and slowed to a trickle the water in his iron kitchen sink. Between his lucrative new work and having to resist his curiosity and rage about Ardoin's new house and "the destroyer," he managed to maintain his equanimity into the fall.

"Where the hell does he float the destroyer?" Pete asked Duke one evening at the bar, as they each sipped on one of Lou's depth charges. A "depth charge" was a quart pitcher of tap beer with a shot glass of rye whiskey dropped in and rolling around on the bottom of the pitcher.

"He takes it up to Caspian and roars around the Lake scaring the shit out of loons and driving local fishermen crazy. You can hear the thing from one end of the lake to the other. Most people who've got camps there would like to torpedo him. He tries to curry favor or show off — I can't tell which — by offering people rides, especially the kids. 'Course, they love ridin' in the damn thing." Pete just shook his head.

After a day grading newly graveled roads in Wolcott and trucking his dozer back to his cabin, Pete stopped off at Lou's for a cooler. Duke was there and the two consumed several of Lou's depth charges. Duke confided in Pete that his friend in the State Police told him they were keeping an eye on Ardoin and had sent a telegram to the Mounties to see if he had any "background."

"Do tell," leered Pete. "What's that snaggle-tooth bastard been up to, anyhow?"

"Don't know yet. I just know they're keepin' an eye out. Seems he prefers givin' boat rides to young boys rather than grown-ups."

"Bas...terd! Sacre bleu! You mean he's a prevert?"

"Don't know. Keep this ta yerself. Don't want ta warn him we'se watchin' him."

After two more depth charges and a warning from Duke to "drive careful," Pete departed Lou's with a peristaltic blast that turned all heads toward the door. It was dark as he headed into his cabin, but the smell of fresh-cut wood and two-cycle engine oil caused him to pause and look around. His newly transplanted popples were lying on the ground in a snowdrift of woodchips. Pete was livid. Seeing lights still on at Ardoin's, he started over to confront him then remembered his friend's admonition. He returned to his cabin to plot his response to this latest insult.

The next morning, the Lincoln left around eleven, towing the destroyer. Pete took his chainsaw over and, within ten minutes, dropped the foundation plantings and crab apples around the property, leaving them where they fell. He then retrieved his key to his neighbor's and went in. Starting in the basement, he threw every other breaker in the breaker box. He then unscrewed the PVC gooseneck cleanout for the sewer drain, stuffed a pair of work gloves into it and replaced the cap. He then stuffed a T-shirt into the dryer vent pipe. He then retrieved from his own house one of the four freshly trapped beavers he was planning to skin, put it in the kitchen oven and set it for 450 degrees. He relocked the house and left. By 1 PM oily smoke was billing from the open windows in Ardoin's bedroom.

Contented, Pete left to collect his check from the Town Clerk. In the office, he again ran into Duke who was looking through land records. Duke suggested they get a coffee at Paine's and the two left in Duke's squad car.

"Doesn't look good," Duke confided before Pete could tell him what had happened to his popples.

"He's got some priors in Quebec. My friend in the state police is just sorting out what's what and he's promised to keep me in the loop. Meanwhile, Gert, up in Greensboro says, he's been giving boat rides to a lot of little boys, but he has 'em all wear bathing suits that he gives them. Whole thing is weird if'n you ask me."

Pete then told Duke that Ardoin hired someone to cut the popples on his property and asked if that wasn't trespassing or malicious something or other? Duke smiled, "You, Pete Trepanier, gonna sue someone for trespassin?" Pete didn't share his amusement.

When Pete got home, Ardoin's house was lit up like an airport, two state troopers, the town pumper truck, and the fire chief's red Jeep Wagoneer. Red and blue revolving beacons lit up the evening sky. When Pete pulled up, a "statie" walked over and asked him if he knew anything about the damage done to Dr. Ardoin's house. Pete said he'd been with Duke that morning. Duke's name commanded both respect and credibility. Pete asked how the trooper thought he might ever have gotten into his neighbor's house, short of breaking a window. He asked if there were any signs of a break-in. Feeling no need to answer Pete's interrogation, the trooper returned toward the scene of the crime.

"Maybe you should be checkin' with the local suckers what signed up to work for him!" Pete yelled at the retreating officer. "Besides," he added, "I plan to go after him for trespassing on my prop'ty and cuttin' my trees down."

The trooper looked back at the downed trees and asked, "You got proof he did that?"

"Who else would? No one else lives anywhere near here and he didn't want 'em blockin' his precious view," Pete finished as he went into his cabin to watch from inside.

The next morning Duke came out early to Pete's house. "I warned you, you asshole, not to get involved," Duke said. "You put that beaver in his oven didn't you."

Pete looked his friend in the eye and denied it outright, adding, "How'd I get in? Place is locked up like the bank."

"If I find you been messin' with Ardoin, I'm gonna have to arrest you. Steer clear, hear me?"

Pete nodded, "I hear ya."

Before long Ardoin was bad-mouthing the locals that built his house, electricity didn't work right, sewer didn't drain properly, and a host of other things were wrong. Pete stuck to his own business, except when Ardoin was off giving boat rides on Caspian.

"Ardoin's been arrested," Duke said to Pete three days later. He was taking boys out for boat rides and then makin' 'em put on little Speedo bathing suits and taking pictures of them changing and he was posin' 'em. State boys got a bunch of Polaroids. There's also a warrant for more serious stuff in Quebec. Wonder how he got across the border."

Pete made no secret of his enthusiasm for this news and celebrated with several more depth charges after Duke left. When word spread of Ardoin's conviction and sentencing — he got eight years followed by extradition to Canada — Pete swung into action.

With Ardoin behind bars, Pete's nearest neighbor was Luke, who lived half a mile up the road in a shack. No one, including Luke, seemed to know his last name. His always empty mail box said "Morris Winslow," presumably an earlier owner.

As Duke said, "Luke's blind in one eye and blind drunk in the other." Every other day, Luke would drive his ramshackle truck in first gear to Averill's Market, buy a case of Old Fitzgerald beer and a yard of McKenzie link franks and then drive home. It was his only sober time of day. He'd set the case up on its end on his front porch and sit on it, extracting a new bottle as needed from between his knees while nibbling on a raw frank with his left hand. When the box collapsed, he'd had enough to go to bed.

Pete stopped by one winter day to bring Luke some more wood for his stove, but couldn't find him. He checked the privy and found Luke in there ice fishing. Luke would hardly be a witness to Pete's plan.

The hardest part was digging a big enough hole; the most fun was driving the big dozer through Ardoin's living room. By morning light, Pete had buried the monstrosity and was grading over the former lawn. He also buried the popple slash and stumps. He spent the rest of the day restoring the landscape it to its former state. He removed all the iron boundary stakes he could find and, just before noon, hit the kill switch on his dozer and went inside to have some coffee and rest.

No word of the interment of his neighbor's house emerged until the following year when the Johnson tax assessors arrived. They had heard there was a house on the remote property, but were left no choice but to assess the land as "undeveloped." Mary Cross, one of the assessors, was delegated to check the town records where she found a building permit that indicated that a house had at least been permitted. Pete remained mum on the subject until Duke confronted him.

"Where's the goddamn house," he asked his friend.

"I buried it," Pete responded.

"Oh, Jesus," Duke gasped.

"I figured I'd be dead before that pervert ever got out of jail."

"You better hope he has no relatives or heirs. I should just arrest you now, you old fool. What in hell were you thinking?"

"That the land looked better without it," answered Pete, acting somewhat hurt at his friend's condescending tone.

"Just keep your mouth shut until I figure this out." Duke said as he left.

The issue resolved itself handily when Pete bought the property from Ardoin's estate for a pittance after he died of a stroke while serving his third year in St Albans Correctional Facility, still facing extradition. Neither the court-appointed estate lawyer nor the real estate appraiser understood or were informed that there had ever been a house there.

Morrisville's First Civil Union

"WHY EVEN HAVE a wedding? June Miller and Bev Labarge have been in a Boston marriage since anyone remembers. Bev teaches kindergarten and June works in the library. Nobody ever fretted over that and everyone knew what it was. What'd they need to get married for anyhow? Civil union... gay marriage? I don't get it. Let 'em keep it ta themselves. Nothing wrong, I 'spect, but no need to be all public 'bout it from my way of thinkin'."

"I 'spect same's true of Wilber and Freddie. They been livin' together on Wilber's father's farm since we was kids. Rumors 'boundin' 'bout them, don't cha know, but no one ever cared much. They's both hard workers and always generous at church. You don't hear anyone rattlin' their dentures about them two boys. Both of 'em, hard workers and kindly, too.

"I always wondered about Jimmy LeDuc. He's a loner and a bit swishy, spends time preenin' hisself and speaks all in esses. He waves his arms around a lot like he's tryin' ta show ya something while he's talkin', like one a 'em fancy-pants TV models demonstratin' a new kitchen tool. Bet he's one too, though I never see'd him with any other men much."

"What you two old chatter-biddies flappin' yer gums about, anyway? Sounds like yer up to no good, gossipin' like two spent hens."

"You behave yourself young man. Just cause y'er an officer of the law doesn't give you any right to be rude to two venerable citizens like Mabel and me. We're just catchin' up on this gay marriage law business, 'bout gays and thespians havin' to get married. Didj'a ever?"

"First, ladies, you'd best get your facts straight. Nobody has ta get married. Nobody has to tell they're homosexuals if they don't want to, and gay women are lesbians. Thespians are the members of the Lamoille County Players over in Hyde Park. If you're gonna gossip, get'cher facts right, hear? I just read a fax from the State's Attorney that lays it all out."

"I s'pose it tells you how to do it, too!"

"No, Miss Jane, it doesn't tell you how to do anything. It just says you can get married like you and Everett did before he passed away."

"Well, you could be more polite, young man! Next thing you know, we'll find out you're one, too! Wouldn't be surprised if you came outta the cellar!"

"Closet... 'came out of the closet' is the term when one let's others know they're gay. You girls are a plague on the verities. Thank the Lord you're not on WDEV. Get your facts straight before you go broadcastin' 'round town."

"You keep a civil tongue, Officer Smarty Pants, or we'll have things to say about you. I remember that prom, and we both know who and what was in your trunk when the trooper stopped you. You better watch your mouth!"

Officer Jenkins smiled and left Mildred and Miss Jane in the booth in Lou's diner, knowing full well what rich nourishment they took from their endless gossip.

*   *   *

"You don't even wanna know what I think," blustered Senator Fred Wessel. "I was as clear in the Senate as I am here at home with my constituents. If you wanna be a homo and you leave others alone and practice whatever they do in their own home, I don't give a damn, I just don't understand why the rest of us have to be subject to the spectacle of their bewitchments. When I was a kid, they were called "inverts," now there's many that call 'em "preverts." I don't give a damn what they do with each other. I just don't want 'em gland-handlers chasin' me or anyone else, trying to be my friend, and what do they need a weddin' for anyway, so they can show off their preversions? We already got enough catch and release marriages as it is. I know a couple a farmers up ta Wolcott ought to be proposin' to their sheep."

"Now, Fred, calm yourself. There's nothin' in the new law that affects you or how you're supposed to behave. It just gives 'em the same rights you and Penny have."

"To be normal? It ain't the business of government to be handin' out rights any more'n it is to be handin' out welfare checks. It's the business of churches. I ain't a churchgoer, but I don't know of any ministers handing out heaven-chits to preverts or lettin' their flocks go hungry. Do you? I ain't goin' to any homo weddings either, here, there, or anywhere!"

"Calm down, Fred. Elmore's a small town and everybody knows everbody. I'm sure Jeanette and Carla just thought it would be a good gesture to invite everyone, so's they could see there ain't no harm in it."

"I ain't calmin'! I'm riled. Next thing you know the state'll be making education and health care rights!"

"Fred, education's already a right. Surely, as a senator, you remember... since about 1785?"

"No one asked me."

"You weren't born."

"Well, I can tell you, if I had been...!"

"I know, Fred. You can either make a decision to go and see what it's all about or just stay home and tend your own business, like you always tell other folks to do. I hear Lester's going."

"Well, I used to think Lester was one, too, 'til he knocked up that chunker in Glover and had to marry her. If he is one, it's gonna be a long sentence!"

*   *   *

"You know, Hilda, I don't see's it's such a bad thing. I had an aunt who spent her whole life with a woman. I don't know if they were lesbians or not, but they spent their whole lives together, and I have a nephew who's a homosexual and says so to anyone who asks. He seems proud of it. He's a good kid. I've known him since he was born, never harmed anyone and did well in school, too. His friends his age don't seem to care much that he's homo either. They treat him like any other. Reverend Pease tried to convert him through prayer and all, but Art would have none of it and said he was happy the way he was. Rev. Pease wouldn't let him come to church anymore. That don't seem right."

"I know, Ralph, Rev. Pease was a pompous jerk and everyone knew it. He was probably one himself secretly and was afraid somebody'd find out and he'd lose his job preaching' and his standin' in the community, which ain't all that great, if you ask me, since Jane walked out on him. Most ministers that I know's happily married and stay that way."

"What I keep wonderin', Hilda, is when they get married like the law says they can now, which one's the husband and which one's the wife? I seen gay men act and even dress all female and I seen some women dress in pants and a man's jacket, speak in a deep voice and act like they's runnin' things. Does 'at mean she's the husband or that he's the wife? I'm not sure I get how it works. I don't even wanna think about what happens in bed and what if they want kids like you and I had?"

"They say that they can adopt 'em like you or me could. Don't seem right, 'cause then you'll just have more homosexuals."

"But Doc Willis told at Rotary that kids was born that way, not raised to be that way. Makes sense to me, 'cause my brother-in-law almost had a conniption when he found out his son, Louis, was one... wanted to take him to Waterbury. It was only after a year or two that my sister got him calmed down so's where he could accept him. Now, they get along well enough and even hunt together again during deer season. Louis's got a boyfriend who's studying up to be a large animal vet.

"Well, so we gonna go to the wedding up in Elmore? Not like we know them that well or anything, but they did invite the whole town to join 'em."

"Let's wait, Hilda, and see. Tune your ear for scuttlebutt to hear who all's going. If the whole town goes, it'd be easier than if only a few shows up."

"That's fine, Ralph, but I bet everyone's waiting to see what everyone else does."

"We'll see."

*   *   *

Jeanette and Carla's wedding took place in the upper pasture of the Levesque farm. Jeanette's father, Alcide, had recently baled a third cutting from his upper and lower meadows off the dirt road that dead-ended on a gentle incline that rose to become Elmore Mountain.

A hand-made sign invited guests to park in the farm's lower meadow. Alcide's red Farmall B tractor, towing a hay wagon, put-putted guests from the parking area to the upper meadow where Jeanette, her father, and Carla had arranged successive arcs of hay bale benches to create a Greek theater that looked down on the lake. The full sun of a cloudless September afternoon shimmered on the lake below and highlighted the white cottages dotting its shore.

Off to the side of the seating area, a 55-gallon drum of water simmered over a small wood-fire in a pit bordered by field stones pilfered from a rubble fence nearby. A four-foot pile of fresh-picked sweet corn lay on the ground by the fire. A picnic table next to it held a dozen boxes of McKenzie link hot dogs, several dozen cellophane bags of Bouyea buns, associated condiments, four pounds of butter, a blue cylinder of Morton Salt, and a pile of sharpened tree branches for roasting hot dogs over the fire. There were also bags of marshmallows for the kids. A motley pack of accompanying dogs sniffed around the table, now under guard by a young neighbor who'd been hired to help people extract their corn with tongs after the ceremony.

Jeanette and Carla had long since given up worrying about whether their pioneer nuptials would be attended by the whole town or just a few curiosity seekers. Their invitation had been made, knowing that Elmore's first gay wedding would elicit a mixed response among its 350 residents. If they had leftovers, Meals on Wheels could always use the extra.

By 2:45, several dozen cars were parked in the lower meadow and the road leading up to the farm indicated a steady stream of arrivals. The wedding was scheduled for three but the arriving traffic and the ferrying up of elderly passengers was barely keeping pace, even though most chose to walk the 200 yards to the upper meadow. Jeanette and Carla decided to simply begin the ceremony when the traffic flow ebbed.

The ceremony was to be conducted by a local Justice of the Peace, Nancy Evans, who was noted and respected for her ability to bring more spirit and dash to her marriage ceremonies than the civil minimum required, often quoting from Rilke, Rumi, Goethe, and Mary Oliver on the subjects of love and commitment.

When the tractor put-put died out and the eight curved rows of hay bales were nearly full, the ceremony began. Miss Evans strode to the front of the impromptu theater and welcomed the crowd. To their surprise, she made no mention of that fact that two people of the same sex were going to be legally married for the first time in Lamoille County but rather began with a quote from Rilke:

Once the realization is accepted that even between
the closest human beings infinite distances continue,
a wonderful living side by side can grow, if they succeed
in loving the distance between them, which makes it
possible for each to see the other whole against the sky.

Miss Evans then invited the couples to come forward along with their families. Jeanette and Carla walked in from the left. Jeanette was wearing a diaphanous white dress with small blue flowers and Carla wore a pale blue linen dress with white flowers. Both carried bouquets of wildflowers. Jeanette's father, Alcide, and her older sister, Elise, stood by her side. Carla's mother, stepfather and younger brothers stood with her.

"Which one's the groom's what I can't figure?" whispered Ralph to Hilda.

"Hush, Ralph. Can't cha see, it don't matter?" whispered Hilda back. "Stop ponderin' and just listen for a change. I think it's beautiful."

The civil ceremony proceeded through the vows. Then Jeanette's sister, Elise, sang an 18th century hymn by Justin Morgan in an ethereal soprano. Carla's youngest brother carefully read a poem he did not understand by the Greek poet Sappho. Miss Evans then invited the newlyweds to embrace one another. There were a few whispered remarks, not all of which were inaudible, given how few in these parts could afford hearing aids, but no one seemed to take offense and a number of heads nodded approval of the proceedings to one another.

"Seemed harmless enough to me. I wish 'em both well and it was a beautiful settin'. I didn't miss the church at all, not even the organ," whispered Miss Jane to her pal Mildred.

Jeanette invited the assembled folks to eat their fill of corn and hot dogs. A fiddle and guitar began a mix of western swing and Irish and French Canadian jigs, reels, and waltzes.

The following week the *News and Citizen* covered the area's first gay marriage, finishing their terse article with their highest accolade for the Elmore event: "And fun was had by all."

Whiskey of the Gods

JACK AND JOSIE Trono live on a sprawling estate in Belvidere, a sparse suburb of the nearby college town, Johnson. Three hundred residents, all living either on Bog Road, Back Road or Basin Road in Belvidere Center, Belvidere Corners or Belvidere Junction live quietly on 32 square miles of forest and bog.

The Trono home expands out from a raised ranch erected in the late '50s by Josie's father, Lester, after he retired from the asbestos mine in Eden. Over the ensuing years his daughter Josie and her common-law husband, Jack, added on to the house to make room for children and edible animals. Not much of a carpenter, Jack simply bought retired semi-trailers and joined them to the main house with flashing, plywood, and tar paper. The three trailers for housing pigs, chickens and two Jerseys each have doorways Jack cut out with his chainsaw. These exits vary in size according to their inhabitants and open into pens fenced in by vertically arranged pallets that Jack gets from the same friend who sold him the trailers. The kids' trailers have no windows, making them easier to heat. One came with a pile of movers' quilts that now insulate the walls of their bedrooms. A complex system of fans keeps heat from the Sam Daniels Furnace moving through the entire complex.

Jack works as a hired-hand on three of the last dairy farms in the area and stays busy during the summer at Gleason's Forage Farm in Lowell, driving tractor and baling hay for sale in Connecticut and New Jersey. Josie takes care of the kids and animals and drives a school bus during the school year. Her Dad, Lester, drinks and occasionally minds the kids. He loves the good whiskey he can no longer afford since he retired and opened his home to his daughter's growing family.

Lester and his buddies used to cross the border late at night on a logging road that ran North from Lake Carmi up to Dunham, Quebec, where

Cécile Frenette would welcome them in the converted garage, now a small bar attached to her home. A shelf over the blue linoleum bar displayed a range of whiskeys from screech to Haig and Haig Pinch, and Seagram's Crown Royal.

Lester loved to sit at the bar with his friends and slowly savor a warm tumbler of Crown Royal while chatting with his friends until it was time to head home again. He now drinks Cadillac Club for $2.60 a bottle, ordering it from Peavine Graves in Morrisville who fetches liquor weekly from the State Store in Waterbury for his Lamoille County patrons.

* * *

Alphonse Lanier lives in Waterbury Center and has a PT-17 Stearman bi-plane he bought at a military auction in 1947 for $1200. After rebuilding and retro-fitting a used 9-cylinder Pratt & Whitney radial engine, he uses it for crop-dusting, joyriding, and the occasional run into Quebec for booze and firecrackers. The 300-horsepower power biplane excels at short-field landing and take-off, so Alphonse keeps a grass strip mowed down the center of the flattest part of his back hayfield for his runway. The only avionics at "Lanier International," as his wife Ruth calls the grass strip and lean-to outback is a windsock she made for him in a clearing beyond the end of the runway. He mounted it on an axle driven into the ground with a wheel bearing and hub that allows the sock to swivel in the wind. Ruth also has a radio in her kitchen on which Alphonse can report his ETAs to her.

Most of Alphonse's business flights are at an elevation of ten feet over apple and pear trees in Addison County and across the Lake in upstate New York. When he comes home, the struts are often festooned with apple branches caught in the crevasse where the tires are attached.

Occasionally, Alphonse gets paid to fly hunters north to Baie Como or Bonaventure for a week of deer, moose, or caribou hunting. The trips he most enjoys, though, are to Saguenay — Jonquière, north of Québec City to fish and hunt with his pal Rufus Denford. But Rufus was shot last year by his wife when she learned he had another wife across the border in Magog.

Mostly now, he flies to Sherbrooke to smuggle back illegal fireworks or booze one can't buy at the State Store. His customers run the gamut from local fish and game clubs to wealthy retirees in Stowe looking for a case or two of exotic Canadian whiskeys. Sometimes, he's just hired for a pleasure ride along the spine of the Green Mountains where he and his passenger fly among the turkey buzzards and eagles gyring in the updrafts. More recently, Alphonse is being hired to tow soaring planes off the tarmac at the new Morrisville-Stowe Airport and bear them aloft to a pre-arranged release at 8-10,000 feet. Crop dusting is a waning business, replaced by genetic engineering.

Alphonse is returning home from a day of golf in Sherbrooke with his Uncle Roger and two cases of Seagram's Crown Royal ordered by the Lake Mansfield Trout Club. As they fly over Derby Line, Alphonse always dips his wing to the border patrol below, even though it is now well after dusk and he is flying without lights, relying on the few instruments on his console. He radios ahead to Ruth to let her know that he'll have to land at the Morrisville-Stowe Airport because of the low cloud cover and to ask her to phone ahead and have Fred turn on the approach lights as he'll be landing in about half an hour. She radios back almost immediately, saying that Fred, the airport manager confirmed that he would, but mentioned that "a couple of staties" had driven up in a cruiser and asked if a certain Alphonse Lanier" had filed a flight plan recently. Fred answered truthfully that he had not, as Alphonse had never filed a flight plan since he left the service and, in fact, left that clear morning from his grass strip unbeknown to Fred. Fred truthfully acknowledged knowing Alphonse, but professed no knowledge of his whereabouts which, at the time of the question was God's honest truth.

Alphonse knows right away what he must do. He yells back to Roger through the voice tube that he'll be doing a slow roll and that Roger has to let drop the two cases sitting at his feet. Alphonse is crestfallen. The profit he'd see from the two cases would cover the cost of his fuel, their green fees, a hearty smoked-meat lunch, and eight Molson Bras d'Ors. He tightens his seat belt and slowly begins to roll the roaring Stearman as it races through the clouds. He is flying low at 5,000 feet, trying to get below the cloud cover, but still can see nothing. He watches through his rear view mirror as first one and then another case of the prized whiskey drops into the clouds. Roger waves at him and slowly the plane rolls back upright and lurches on into the night. Roger begins his descent almost immediately and sooner than expected sees the red hazard beacons flashing in the distance indicating his approach into the airport. The landing lights are on as Fred promised, and Alphonse touches down gently and taxies the biplane up to the small trailer that serves as an office when anyone's on duty.

Alphonse sees the cruiser and watches as two state policemen approach his plane. The motor sputters to a close and the propeller kicks several times before finally bouncing to rest. Alphonse hops over the side and greets the two men.

"Hello, boys, what's up? Need to rent me and Ol' Yeller, here?"

"Alphonse Lanier?"

"That's me and this here's my Uncle Roger. We been golfin' all day up ta Sherbrooke. How can we help?"

"Can we look in your plane? We're checking on a report that you might be carrying illegal goods across the border."

"Help yourself. There's no cargo space in that beast except the dust tanks and they're empty. Don't crop dust at night... too risky."

The policemen climb up the side step, lean over into both cockpits with their flashlights, and in short order, convince themselves there's no contraband on board.

"Sorry to bother you Mr. Lanier, we got an anonymous report that you might be carrying contraband. Be careful! Ever since those plastic-covered bales of marijuana were found bobbing around in Lake Memphremagog, we've had to step up surveillance."

"Thanks gentlemen, I read about that, but I don't move drugs."

"Be careful now... loved the fireworks you got for us down in Pittsford, by the way," the corporal says with a broad wink.

The next morning, Lester pours some coffee into his big ironstone mug that Josie always leaves on the woodstove to heat up before she heads out to plug in the block-heater in the Bluebird school bus parked in the yard. Jack has no work and a mild hangover, so he sleeps in. Lester grabs his mug and the white enamel bucket of last night's leftovers and heads out to the chicken coop to feed his biddies. To his surprise, the cool morning air is richly perfumed with the smell of whisky. It's a deep peaty smell, the kind he associates not with the rotgut he's had to contend with since he retired, but rather with the fragrant sippin' whiskeys he used to enjoy at Cécile's.

At first, he thinks the breeze must have caught some trace of a neighbor making corn whiskey. Then he spots the drenched cardboard box sitting over by the old outhouse. He sets his coffee on a fence post and walks over to see what's in the box. As soon as he pulls the cardboard apart, he realizes the familiar smell came from the missile someone dropped from on high next to the shitter. It looks like it fell a long way, as all the bottles are broken except two that have somehow escaped the impact. He picks through the drenched corrugated and cullet, savoring the redolence of fine whisky.

It seems like a cruel joke of whatever gods are up there that they'd deliver a shattered case of his favorite whiskey so roughly, but he's grateful for the two survivors and stashes them away for quiet sips when he's alone.

Lester tips the pail of slops to the eager hens and listens to them gabble and comment about the contents of their first meal of the day. He continues over to the pigsty to grain "the bacon," as Jodie called her two prize Durocs. From there, he goes on to refill the washtub with water for her two Jerseys.

As he walks past the manure pile that grows larger each passing year, since no one's spent the energy to spread it anywhere, he sees another cardboard case jutting from the side of the pile. He rushes over and pulls it from the deep cavity it's made in the soft pile of wet manure. It's an unbroken case of Seagram's Crown Royal. He looks up to the sky to ponder where these cases fell from or what bacchanalian deity dropped them into his life... fourteen bottles of his favorite whiskey. At the rate he'll sip it, it'll last him to the grave. He spends the rest of the day wondering who might come into his life that will share his love of these beautiful whiskeys.

Dead Coon

HEDLEY JESSUP GOT his new start in Stowe after a series of events which had largely depleted him. First, he lost his job on the *Herald Tribune*. He'd been on the city desk for three years when the *Tribune* went into a precipitous decline and was acquired by the *New York Times*. The editorial staffers not invited into the Gray Lady's international newsroom were left holding an empty bag of journalism degrees and beat credentials.

Martha Mosley-Jessup, sensing no material future in their marriage, left Hedley for an older aristocrat in the investment bank Kuhn Loeb. Her material aspirations, satisfied for the succeeding decade, again were brought low when her alcoholic banker-husband didn't survive the merger with Lehmann Brothers in 1977. At this point Hedley lost track of his first wife but was enjoying tryouts for a new wife in his new Stowe A-frame.

Hedley was not a skier, but was open to becoming one after he secured a reporter position at the area's long-time paper-of-record, *The News and Citizen*. Although his new job paid less than half of what he had made at the *Herald Tribune*, his expenses were half of what they'd been in Manhattan where he had paid $94 a month for a two-bedroom apartment on East 95th Street on the edge of Harlem.

At first, he struggled to forget the amenities he associated with Manhattan, like Sunday brunch at a Mannie's delicatessen on 86th Street where he'd savor a potato knish and two cups of creamy coffee while reading the *New York Times* Sunday edition. The Saturday matinee at the Film Forum and his evening bottle of Merlot were also missing from his new start in Stowe. But, in time, he came to appreciate his proximity to nature, the sweeping vistas from Stowe Hollow, and his anticipation of a sunny and verdant spring.

The weekly *News and Citizen* made fewer demands on his time than had the daily *Herald Tribune*. He gratefully forgot the *Herald*'s style manual in favor of the native language of local news with its own lexicon that he came to learn with the help of the paper's owner-editor, Clyde Limoge.

The old style manual's "avoid the passive voice," became in the *News and Citizen* its signature, "fun was had by all." Clyde often knew his audience better than they knew themselves and maintained a twinkle in his eye and his news stories.

One amenity, Hedley determined not to forego was a housekeeper. His former wife Martha disdained housework and Hedley was useless at domestic chores, so they had always kept a housekeeper. Even after Martha disappeared without notice, he kept on "Rita," even though he could no longer afford her.

After settling into his new home in Stowe, he ran an ad in his employer's classifieds for a weekly cleaning lady to keep his new home tidy. He got three responses. One was an elderly French-Canadian woman who had just lost her husband and wept throughout the interview, even as she finished a plate of Fig Newton cookies sitting on his dinette table. The second was a feisty woman named Denise in her late 30s. She began the interview with a long list of "just-so-you-know, I don'ts...," that ended with "sleep around." Most of the things she refused to do never occurred to him as part and parcel of keeping house, so her demurrals didn't matter. As long as she would clean the porcelain fixtures in his bathroom, run laundry, clean the fridge, mop floors, and vacuum rugs, he would be content. The third woman didn't show. Denise was to report to work the following Monday morning and work until noon. She charged $1.75 an hour.

After settling into the relaxed pace of helping produce a weekly local filled with items such as new business start-ups, farm commodity prices, weddings, funerals; car, farm, and ski accidents, and the journalistic confetti of local social event reporting, Hedley resumed his own social life, attending local events in Stowe and Morrisville, making the rounds of Stowe's nightlife, and eventually meeting a woman also "in the game" as he liked to say. She'd moved up from New Jersey where she'd worked for eight years in human resources for Chubb Insurance after graduating from the University of Vermont. She missed Vermont and, most especially, the winter ski weekends in Stowe and Smugglers Notch. She longed to be skiing with pals again and for the nightlife that followed a hard day of skiing.

Ellen and Hedley began with quiet meals together in town. Ellen finally succeeded in getting Hedley on a pair of rented skis and spent three weekends urging him patiently down the Toll House practice slope.

He mastered the snowplow, then a few stem Christies and finally succeeded in keeping his skis parallel. His biggest challenge was the rope tow
itself, especially in early spring when the wet hemp burned through his
leather mittens as he tried in vain to tighten his grip on the careening rope.

Hedley's first serious domestic challenge developed when a horde of
raccoons found their bliss around his A-frame. He first spotted them wad-
dling around at dusk one night looking as if they'd lost something important. The long trays of geranium pots lining the deck railing of his A-frame
resisted bloom until Ellen suggested he add bone meal to the soil. Just as
the geraniums began to green up and bloom out, he came down one morning to find piles of terra cotta shards, scattered soil and broken geranium
stems.

"Must a been 'em coons," commented Denise as she surveyed the
wreckage with a broom and snow shovel. "Said you put some bone meal in
'em pots. That's like planting apple trees in your living room for the deer.
Works fine if your aim is to shoot a buck, but 'em coons smells food even
where there ain't none. I jess use chemicals to fertilize my germaniums.
Coons hate Miracle Glo or whatever it's called."

Meanwhile, Ellen and Hedley's relationship had graduated to sleep-
overs in the A-Frame.

Several weeks later Hedley picked his way down the narrow spiral
staircase from the sleeping loft to find the lower screen of his deck door
pushed in and two chubby raccoons at the bowl of kittie-kibble he left for
his tabby, Rufus. Rufus, sitting in a kush position under the dinette table,
kept a wary eye on the interlopers honking down his breakfast.

"That's it! I've had it. I gotta find someone to get rid of these goddamn
raccoons."

Hedley grabbed a broom, perhaps for the first time ever, and began
swatting the animals toward the screen door. The raccoons, looking hurt,
seemed not to understand Hedley's eviction since it was clear to everyone
including Rufus, they hadn't finished their meal.

Hedley relied on his boss, Clyde, and less often on Denise for advice on
country living matters.

"Shoot the bastards," laughed Clyde as he listened to Hedley complain
about the coons rampaging through his garbage cans and potted plants,
and making themselves at home in his kitchen. There's way too many

of them, like the goddamn beaver back-flooding and drowning out the hardwoods."

"I've never shot anything before and don't even own a gun," protested Hedley.

"And you from New York City...no gun? You call me next time they show up and I'll dispatch 'em... bring my 12-gauge."

"Seriously?" asked Hedley.

"Sure, just ring me at home, 4476, and I'll be over. Coons usually work in teams."

Ellen worked weekdays at The Mountain Company, handling personnel matters for their hospitality employees. On weekends she skied with or without Hedley and now spent most evenings in his sleeping loft. It was President's Day weekend and the celebration of national holidays had recently been moved to Mondays to allow for three-day weekends.

Saturday of that weekend had been particularly bad. Hedley's garbage had been re-sorted in the night into piles covering most of the driveway in front of his attached breezeway garage. Three more frozen pots lay shattered on the deck and as Hedley inspected the wreckage, he spotted two raccoons peering over the gunwales in his new wooden rowboat on which they'd been chewing.

Hedley called Clyde who arrived minutes later with his shotgun and a pocket full of turkey loads.

"Them bastards love the taste of wood glue for some reason, probably the casein. They did the same thing to my duck boat and blind. Had to daub the whole thing with creosote to keep 'em off'n it. We gotta lure 'em off the boat so I don't blow it to bits with 'em. Go get some bread or crackers.

Hedley returned with a handful of graham crackers and Clyde tossed them in front of the coons, but away from Hedley's rowboat. The coons trundled over the side and waddled over to inspect Clyde's offering when a single loud blast knocked both of them on their sides and splintered the crackers. Their feet continued moving in a futile effort at escape. Thirty seconds later, they went still, Clyde walked over and kicked them over to be sure they were dead. "You bury this one. I'm settin' the other up as a warning."

Hedley got his only shovel, a large aluminum snow shovel, and tried to push its broad edge into the hardened snowbank while Clyde picked up the other coon and carried him up onto the deck where he arranged him carefully on the railing next to the few frozen flower pots.

"Let this be a warnin' to ya... bastards... Won't see any more coons on this deck for awhile. Just leave 'im here till spring when he thaws out, then you can bury him with his buddy."

"Course you may not finish that hole yer diggin 'til spring with that shovel... ain't easy digging soil that's froze-up solid with a snow shovel, is it? Ain't cha got a roundhead shovel?"

"This is the only shovel I got," said Hedley. "Denise got it for me at Stowe Hardware. She doesn't shovel snow."

"I 'spect not," answered Clyde with a smile. " 'At ain't all she don't do neither... many's tried. I got a shovel and crow bar in my pickup."

Clyde dug a hole and kicked the raccoon into it with his boot and buried it back up.

"Gotta go, Polly's havin' a clutch of biddies over for tea and strumpets and I wanna be in deep in the woods when they arrive."

Clyde set his gun on the floor against the passenger seat, tossed his shovel in the back of the truck and roared off giving Hedley a goodbye wave.

Hedley looked with confusion at the raccoon curled up on the deck railing and shook his head wondering if he would ever understand country ways.

Ellen couldn't visit Saturday night, but the two spent Sunday skiing at Spruce Peak. It was Hedley's first chairlift ride and he looked anxiously at how high he was above the ground and the distance from the top of Spruce Peak to the base lodge. He saw how narrow the trails leading down were. So far, he'd only skied on wide practice slopes and relied on the width of a practice slope to traverse back and forth without gaining too much speed. Ellen, however, deemed him ready for trail skiing and chose the intermediate Sterling for his first run.

To his surprise, he enjoyed the trip down and felt more comfortable than he had expected, as he crisscrossed the wide trail during his descent and appreciated the supportive comments from his new girlfriend.

That night the two shared a bottle of Hedley's treasured Merlot and to his delight, Ellen was able to spend the night, as Monday was a holiday and she had the day off. Hedley, however, had to go into the office in the morning to edit several stringer pieces intended for Wednesday's paper and so Ellen slept in and then later headed for the slopes alone.

Hedley returned from work around mid-afternoon that Monday, having completely forgotten that Denise didn't recognize national holidays, only religious ones, and thus had spent the morning cleaning his A-frame. When he sat down at the kitchen dinette, he saw her note:

> *Mr. Jessup,*
> *Leave my money in your mailbox and*
> *I'll fetch it tomorrow before the postman comes.*
> *Like your new woman.*
> *Dead coon on the deck.*
> *Denise.*

CPSIA information can be obtained
at www.ICGtesting.com
Printed in the USA
BVHW041500290323
661367BV00005B/640